"Play with me. It'll be fun."

Taking Josie's hands, he placed them around his neck. His hands low on her hips, he swayed her in time to the music.

"Dallas…"

"You look awfully cute in that robe." He especially liked her messy pile of crazy-corkscrew hair. How the deep V at her throat guided his eyes to naughty places.

"I'm thirty-three. Hardly in the right age bracket for cute."

"Says who?" Cinching her close enough that even air couldn't squeeze between them, he nuzzled her neck.

She made a halfhearted effort to push him away, but then he slipped his hand beneath her chin, drawing her lips to his. Their kiss was awkward and tender and the most exciting thing to happen to him in years.

Dear Reader,

Last we "talked" my kiddos were graduating from high school. Now, they're setting off for college. Where did the time go? Aside from my achy "rain" knee, I don't feel any older. Lord knows, most days our kids don't act older! LOL! So why are we now packing up their bedrooms to launch them into the world?

In Dallas and Josie's story, Dallas is a single father to naughty twins, which gave me plenty of time to reflect over our own twin mischief. Our daughter refused to cook in her play kitchen with fake food, so I was constantly finding the milk, eggs and cheese in her room! Our son could take his room from neat-as-a-pin to ransacked in under thirty minutes. Finally, I gave up on sorting Legos, Lincoln Logs, army guys and dinosaurs into their own neat bins. Giant tubs were much easier to shovel the mess into!

At each stage of raising our children, Hubby and I were convinced that that was the toughest we'd have it. Just as Dallas feels kindergarten is hard, fourth grade science fair projects kicked our behinds. Now that our kids will soon be leaving the nest, we're thinking the hardest parenting task of all is saying goodbye.

Lucky for Dallas, he's got a few more years before that happens. What he doesn't have is the willpower to steer clear of Josie, the girls' pretty teacher!

Happy reading!

Laura Marie

The Rancher's Twin Troubles

LAURA MARIE ALTOM

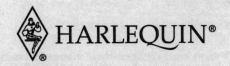

HARLEQUIN®

TORONTO • NEW YORK • LONDON
AMSTERDAM • PARIS • SYDNEY • HAMBURG
STOCKHOLM • ATHENS • TOKYO • MILAN • MADRID
PRAGUE • WARSAW • BUDAPEST • AUCKLAND

Recycling programs
for this product may
not exist in your area.

ISBN-13: 978-0-373-75346-8

THE RANCHER'S TWIN TROUBLES

Copyright © 2011 by Laura Marie Altom

www.eHarlequin.com

Printed in U.S.A.

ABOUT THE AUTHOR

After college (Go Hogs!), bestselling, award-winning author Laura Marie Altom did a brief stint as an interior designer before becoming a stay-at-home mom to boy/girl twins and a bonus son. Always an avid romance reader, she knew it was time to try her hand at writing when she found herself replotting the afternoon soaps.

When not immersed in her next story, Laura teaches art at a local middle school. In her free time, she beats her kids at video games, tackles Mount Laundry and of course reads romance!

Laura loves hearing from readers at either P.O. Box 2074, Tulsa, OK 74101, or email BaliPalm@aol.com.

Love winning fun stuff? Check out
www.lauramariealtom.com!

Books by Laura Marie Altom

HARLEQUIN AMERICAN ROMANCE

This story is dedicated to all of the friends
who've helped raise our kids.
We couldn't have done it without you!

Special thanks to Tom and Karen Gilbert, Lynne and
Tony Beeson, Susie Thornbrugh, Kim Blackketter,
Jennifer Crutchfield, Jackie and John Butts, Karen
and Jack Lairmore, and Melinda and Scott Taylor.

This list is woefully incomplete, but to fill it,
I'd need a dedication book, rather than page!

Chapter One

"Are we talking about the same kids?" Dallas Buck-horn shifted on the pint-size chair in his twin daughters' kindergarten classroom. Across a sea of tiny tables, his angels made dinner in a play kitchen. "Because my Betsy and Bonnie wouldn't pull a stunt like that."

Uptight Miss Griffin folded her hands atop her desk, full lips pressed into a frown. Her mess of red curls had escaped the clip at the back of her neck, making her look more like a pretty teen ditching school than a full-grown woman teaching it. "While the girls are lucky to have such wonderful support in their corner, the fact remains that our classroom fish tank had an entire package of Kool-Aid spilled in."

"Yes, well—" the tank's purple-tinged water forced Dallas to hide a chuckle "—the goldfish don't seem to mind."

"Since you seem to find this amusing, Mr. Buckhorn, you should know that at the time of the incident, your girls were the only children near the tank."

"Yeah, but did you see them do it?"

After a moment's hesitation, she said, "No, but—"

Dallas stood. "Ever heard the phrase 'innocent until proven guilty'?"

"Sir, with all due respect, this isn't the first time I've had trouble with the girls. They've put popcorn in the plants to see if it would grow. Sneaked cafeteria food into our play kitchen and served it to other students. The last time it rained, they—"

"Whoa." Slapping on his Stetson, Dallas said, "I don't know what you're trying to prove, but *if* Bonnie and Betsy did all of that, sounds to me like my babies aren't getting adequate supervision. Maybe you're the one who needs looking after?"

On her feet, hand on her hips, she said, "I've been teaching for ten years, and trust me, I understand it must be hard hearing your children are, well…out of control, but—"

Dallas whistled for his girls and they came running. "Did you two do that to the fish tank?" He pointed at the purple mess.

"No, Daddy," they said in unison, big blue eyes wholly innocent.

"There you have it." Hands on their backs, he ushered them to the classroom's door. The smell of crayons and paste was bringing on a headache. Clearly, the teacher must've been sniffing too much of that white school glue. "My girls said they're not guilty. End of story. Before we go, want help switching out the water?"

"HE DIDN'T?"

"Oh, he did." Josie put a carrot stick to her mouth and chomped. The teachers' lounge was blessedly quiet.

Josie had a free period while her kiddos were in music class, and she was enjoying every minute with her best friend, Natalie Stump. "Then he and the girls cleaned out the tank. Does that sound like something the father of innocent children would do?"

"No…" Natalie struggled opening a chocolate milk carton. "But it was decent of him. Maybe he has issues with admitting his daughters are anything less than perfect." As Weed Gulch Elementary School's counselor, Natalie was always on the hunt for the best in people. Usually it was a trait Josie found endearing, but in this case, already dreading the twins' next stunt, she wished Dallas Buckhorn would wake up and see the delinquents he was raising.

Josie sighed. "Bonnie and Betsy are adorable and funny and smart, but both have an ornery streak I can't control."

Without thinking, Josie took Natalie's milk carton and had it open in a flash.

"You're good at that."

"I'm pretty sure I had a college course on stubborn milk."

"Nothing on tough-to-handle kids though, huh?"

"More than I can count, but these two beat anything I've ever seen. If they continue this trend, by third grade they'll be robbing ice cream trucks."

Natalie chuckled. "They're not *that* bad."

"Mark my words. This isn't the last time I'll have to confront their father."

"At least he's hot." Natalie poked Josie in the ribs

with an elbow. "Makes for interesting parent/teacher conferences."

Heat crept up Josie's neck. *Hot* was hardly the word. The man was more in the realm of drop-dead gorgeous, but that was beside the point. "He's all right. If you go for that sort." Tall, spiky dirty-blond hair, faded jeans that hugged his—

"Don't even try lying to me. That porcelain skin of yours gives everything away. You're blushing."

"Am not." Josie had always hated her pale complexion, and this was just one more reason why.

The late September day was warm and she dumped her last two baby carrots in the trash, preferring to stand in front of the window air-conditioning unit, letting the cool wash away her crabby mood.

"Let's hope," Natalie said, thankfully off the subject of the all-too-handsome cowboy, "this conference will serve as a wake-up call for the girls. I bet you don't have a lick of trouble from now to the end of the year."

"BETSY! BONNIE! GET DOWN from there before you break every bone in your little bodies!" Beneath the mammoth arms of an oak that'd no doubt been on the playground since before Oklahoma had even been a state, Josie stared up at the Buckhorn twins. How had they scrambled so high? Especially so fast? The first branch was a good five feet from the ground. She'd cautioned the three teachers on playground duty to keep a close watch on the twins, but they reported that the girls had been too quick for anyone to stop them.

"Look at me!" Bonnie shouted, hanging upside down monkey-style at least fifteen feet in the sweltering air.

"I can do it, too!" Betsy shouted, much to Josie's horror, mimicking her sister's stunt. It'd only been a week since Josie's meeting with their dad and already they were finding mischief.

Winded, Natalie approached. "I called their father and he's on his way. Luckily, I caught him on his cell and he's already in town."

"Thanks," Josie said. "Obviously, the girls aren't listening to any of us. Maybe he can talk them down."

"I'm flying!" Bonnie shouted, holding out her arms Wonder Woman-style.

"I wanna try," said pigtailed Megan Brown who gazed at her classmate with wide-eyed awe.

"Me, too!" All of a sudden at least twenty of the thirty-eight kindergarteners outside stormed the tree base. Jumping up and down, they looked more like a riotous mosh pit than normally well-behaved children at recess.

"Bonnie, please," Josie reasoned, hand to her forehead shading her eyes from the sun. "Halloween's almost here and you wouldn't want to ruin your costume with a big cast, would you?"

"Casts are cool!" Jimmy Heath declared. "I broke my leg sledding and Dad painted it camo."

"Ooh…" was the crowd consensus.

Josie prayed for calm.

What she got was a black truck hopping the parking lot curb to drive right up onto the playground. At the wheel? Dallas Buckhorn. Lord, how she was well on her way to despising the man. If only he'd taken her seriously during their conference, maybe this wouldn't be happening.

"Come on, kids," Natalie and the other teachers on duty called, gathering the children a safe distance away.

Dallas positioned the truck bed beneath the girls before killing the engine.

Exhaust stung Josie's nose, causing her to sneeze.

"Bless you," he said with a grin and a tip of his hat.

"Daddy!" Betsy cried, waving and swinging. "Look what I can do!"

"I see you, squirrel." He didn't look the least bit disturbed. "Now, before you give your teacher a heart attack, how about you two scramble down from there and into the truck bed."

"Do we have to?" Bonnie asked. "I thought you said it was good for us to climb trees?"

"It is, but that's at home. My guess is that around here, shimmying up things taller than you breaks more than a few rules." Wearing faded jeans, weathered boots, a red plaid Western shirt and his trademark hat, the man looked nothing like a father. More like a cowboy straight off the range.

Natalie leaned over and whispered, "He's so handsome it hurts to look at him."

"Hush," Josie snapped. "This is a serious situa—"

Before she could finish, the girls had scurried down the tree and into the truck bed. Legs rubbery with relief, Josie finally dared to breathe.

"See?" Hat in hand, Dallas sauntered over. His walk

was slow and sexy. "My girls are expert climbers. I don't even know why you called."

Stunned by his cavalier attitude, she wasn't sure what to say. "Do you realize that if either of your girls had fallen from that height, they could've been seriously injured?" Focusing on maintaining a professional demeanor, Josie folded her arms and adopted her best stern-teacher expression.

"Do you realize my angels have been climbing trees practically since they could walk? I've taught them to look out for weak branches and to always plan a safe path down." Checking his truck to find the girls surrounded by their friends, he added, "I've done some of my best thinking in an old oak—at least back when I was a teen."

Shaking her head, she struggled for the right words. "You have to understand that at school, there has to be a certain order to our days. There are procedures and rules to follow—not just for safety, but for learning. By condoning your daughters' actions, you've essentially told every student out here that disobeying my rules and those of the other teachers is not only perfectly okay, but heroic."

"Aren't you exaggerating just a tad?" When he held his thumb and forefingers together, he winked. Despite the fact that he was handsome enough to make her swoon, she held her ground. The man was impossible and he brought out the worst in her. She was never this much of a shrew. But she'd also never encountered someone quite so blind. As young as the twins were, now was the time to temper them. Not in their teens when they were already lost.

"No, sir," she said, standing her ground. "I don't believe I am."

"Then where does that leave us?"

Us? She rationally knew he meant their parent/teacher relationship, but the way he'd slapped his hat back on his head, hooking his thumbs into his back pockets had her distracted. What was wrong with her? Why was it that whenever she came within five feet of him her mind turned to mush and her body fairly hummed? She was finished with men, so why wouldn't her body obey?

"Um…" Josie cleared her throat. "Perhaps you might want to spend time in the classroom with the girls. You'd be able to see what's expected of them, and then pass along the message."

Blanching, he said, "Me? Back in school? No, thanks. Tell you what I will do, though. The girls and I will have a nice, long talk about no more recess tree climbing."

"I'd appreciate it," Josie said, unsure what to do with her hands.

Thankfully, seeing how most of her class had joined the twins in the bed of Dallas's truck, she had more pressing matters than the study of how his hat brim's shadow darkened his eyes.

"Mom," Dallas said that night, chopping an onion for her famous spaghetti sauce, "I swear that woman's going to drive me off the deep end."

Georgina Buckhorn sighed. "How can you be intimidated by a scrap of a kindergarten teacher?"

"Who said I was intimidated?" Dallas brought the knife down especially hard on the onion. The clap of metal hitting the wooden cutting board echoed in the big country kitchen. "She annoys me, that's all."

"Because she speaks the truth and you don't want to hear it?" Her back to him, she took pasta from an upper shelf. She was a tall woman made all the more imposing by the top knot she'd formed with her long silver hair. Once upon a time, before Dallas lost Bobbie Jo, his mother's words had been gold. Now, Dallas resented her for getting into his parenting business. It wasn't that they didn't get along, but where the girls were concerned, they no longer shared the same values.

She always nagged him about the twins needing more discipline, but to his way of thinking, wasn't losing their mother enough? Bobbie Jo had died giving them life. Her last whispered words had been for him to put his love for her into their babies. By God, every day since, that was exactly what he'd done.

Bonnie and Betsy were his world and no one—not his mom and certainly not their teacher—was going to tell him he was a bad parent when his life was dedicated to their happiness.

"Dallas," his mother said, dropping pasta into a pot of already boiling water on the industrial-size stove, "this house is big enough that we can generally keep to our own business, but this is one matter on which I refuse to bend. Sunday night, I caught Betsy drawing all over her bathroom mirror with lipstick. *My* brand-new Chanel lipstick I bought last time we were in Tulsa. When I asked her to help clean the mess, she crossed her arms, raised her chin and flat out told me, 'no.' Now, does that sound reasonable to you?"

After dumping diced onions into a pan filled with Italian sausage, he took the cutting board and knife to the sink, running them both under water.

"Ignore me all you want, but deep down, you know I'm right." Behind him, her hand on his shoulder, she added, "A large part of being a good parent is sometimes being the bad guy. You have to set boundaries. Just like your father and I did with you and your brothers."

"That's different. We were all hell on horseback."

She snorted. "Like your girls are any different because they're only riding the ponies you gave them for Christmas?"

"They love those cuties." He bristled. "Ponies topped the twins' Santa lists."

"Doesn't make it right." She stirred the meat and onions that'd started to sizzle above a gas flame. "Clint Eastwood topped my wish list, but you don't see me out gallivanting, do you?"

"You're impossible." His back turned, he took his work coat from the peg mounted alongside the back door. "I'm going to check the cattle."

"Mark my words, Dallas Buckhorn, you might temporarily hide from this situation, but sooner or later you have to deal with your rambunctious girls."

"GOT IT! AND IT ONLY TOOK ten strokes." Friday evening, on hole seven of Potter's Putt-Putt, Natalie performed a little dance that revealed she may have had one too many beers. It was the monthly ladies' night and judging by the slew of high scores, none of the foursome would give the LPGA a run for their money any time soon.

First grade teacher, Shelby Foster, pushed the counselor aside. "Let me show you how a professional does it…"

"Professional what?" Cami Vettle, the school secretary teased in a raunchy tone.

For the first time in what felt like weeks, Josie truly laughed and it felt not only good, but long overdue. Until just now, she hadn't realized how much stress she'd been under. She'd always loved her job. As a general rule, kindergarteners were a lovable, trouble-free bunch. Oh, sure, she'd dealt with plenty of mischief, but nothing as regular and confounding as the stunts of Betsy and Bonnie Buckhorn.

"You all right?" Natalie asked while waiting for the other women to take their turns.

"Sure," Josie said, swirling her plastic cup of beer. "Why wouldn't I be?" White lights decorated the course's trees. With temperatures in the seventies, it felt as if fall had finally arrived. Shrieks of laughter mingled with top-forty music blaring from loudspeakers. The mouthwatering scent of the snack bar's trademark barbecue normally would have her stomach growling. Lately, though, she'd been so consumed with dreaming up a delicate way to manage the twins that she forgot to eat.

"You seem awfully quiet. Man trouble?" Tipsy,

Natalie leaned on Josie's shoulder. Beer mingled with her pretty floral perfume, again causing Josie's lips to curve into a smile.

"Oh, sure. As you full well know, I haven't been with a man since Lyle, and he was a disaster."

"Only because you didn't put an ounce of effort into the relationship. It's been four years since Hugh died. He wouldn't want you to be lonely."

Then why had he left her?

"Who said I am?" Josie swigged her beer. "And who are you to talk? When's the last time you went on a date?"

"Two weeks ago, thank you very much."

"Your turn," Cami said to Josie, writing down her score. "What are you two gossiping about?"

"Nat, here, says she had a date." Josie centered the ball on the putting mat before giving it a swat. It landed between a giant plaster frog and a rubber lily pad. "You believe her?"

"Absolutely. It was with the UPS man. I witnessed him asking her in the front office."

"Impressive…" Josie's shot landed her ball ten feet from the moat's dragon. Sighing, she stepped over a second lily pad to set up for stroke three.

"Kind of like Betsy and Bonnie's dad. Whew." Cheeks flushed, Cami fanned herself with the score-card. "He's gorgeous."

"Don't look now, but he's also headed this way…" Natalie downed the rest of her beer.

Upon meeting Dallas's penetrating stare, Josie hit her ball all the way to Hansel and Gretel's cottage on hole fourteen!

Chapter Two

"Ladies…" Dallas tipped his hat to Bonnie and Betsy's teacher and three other women he'd seen around the girls' school. "Nice night to be on the links."

The tall brunette laughed at his joke.

"Miss Griffin?" He was intrigued by the notion that she found it necessary to hide behind a pine.

"Please," she mumbled, ducking out from behind a particularly full bough to extend her hand, "outside of school you can call me Josie."

When their fingers touched, he was unprepared for the breeze of awareness whispering through him. It'd been so long since he'd noticed any woman beyond casual conversation that he abruptly released her. Just as hastily broke their stare. Had she felt that shift from the ordinary, too?

"Hi, Miss Griffin!" The twins and three of their more giggly friends danced around him.

"H-hi, girls," their teacher said. Had she always been so hot? Maybe it was the course's dim lighting, but her complexion glowed as pretty as his mama's Sunday pearls. Her hair hung long and wild, and she wore the hell out of a pair of faded jeans and a University of Oklahoma sweatshirt. Red cowboy boots peeked out from beneath her hems. "You all having a party?"

Bonnie nodded. "Daddy's letting us have a sleepover for doing good on our chores all week."

"Congratulations," their teacher said, patting Bonnie's back. "I'm proud of you."

His daughter beamed.

Feeling damned proud for having raised such a conscientious sweetheart, Dallas couldn't help but grin.

"Come on, Daddy." Betsy yanked his arm. "Let's play."

"Well…" Oddly reluctant to end the conversation, Dallas said, "Guess I'd better get going. My bosses are calling."

The look Josie Griffin shot him was painful. As if she disapproved of his play on words. The notion annoyed him and brought him back to the reality of who she was in the grand scheme of things. A teacher he'd never see again after his girls' kindergarten graduation. As for his musings on her good looks? A waste of time he wouldn't be repeating.

"I KNOW, KITTY, THE MAN'S infuriating, isn't he?" While Josie's calico performed figure eights between her legs, she spooned gourmet cat food onto a china saucer. Her friends thought she was nutty for lavishing so much attention on her pet, but Kitty had been a wedding gift from Hugh. When she one day lost her furry friend, she didn't know what she'd do. In some ways, it would be like losing her husband all over again.

Another thing her friends nagged her about was worrying over events that hadn't happened. But surviving the kinds of things Josie had taught her to never underestimate any signs—no matter how seemingly insignificant.

"Kitty," she said, setting the saucer on the wide-planked walnut floor, "do you think when it comes to the Trouble Twins I'm looking for problems where there are none?"

Chowing down on his Albacore Tuna Delight, Kitty couldn't have cared less.

Josie took a banana from the bowl she kept filled with seasonal fruit. Usually in her honey-gold kitchen with its granite counters, colorful rag rugs and green floral curtains, she felt warm and cozy. Content with her lot in life. Yes, she'd faced unspeakable tragedy early on, but as years passed, she'd grown accustomed to living on her own. She shopped Saturday morning yard sales for quilting fabric and took ballet every Thursday night. Even after three years, she was the worst in her class, but the motions and music were soothing—unlike her impromptu meeting with Dallas Buckhorn.

Her hand meeting his had produced the queerest sensation. Lightning in a bottle. Had it been her imagination? A by-product of beer mixed with moonlight? Or just Nat's gushing praise of the man's sinfully good looks catching like a virus?

ON MONDAY MORNING, as calmly as possible, Josie fished for the green snake one of her darlings had thoughtfully placed in her desk drawer. Finally grabbing hold of him—or her—she held it up for her class's squealing perusal. "Don't suppose any of you lost this?"

Bonnie Buckhorn raised her hand. "Sorry. He got out of my lunch bag."

"Yes, well, come and get him and—" Josie dumped yarn from a nearby plastic tub, and then set the writhing snake inside. "Everyone line up. We're taking a field trip."

"Where? Where?" sang a chorus of hyper five-year-olds.

Bonnie took the tub.

"We're going to take Bonnie's friend outside—where he belongs."

"You're not letting him go!" Bonnie hugged the yellow tub, vigorously shaking her head.

"Yes, that's exactly what we're going to do. Now, I need this week's light buddies to do their job, please."

Sarah Boyden and Thomas Quinn scampered out of line to switch off the front and back fluorescent lights.

"Please, ma'am," Betsy said while her twin stood beneath the American and Oklahoman flags crying, "Bonnie didn't mean to put Green Bean in your desk."

"Then how did he get there?" Josie asked as Sarah and Thomas rejoined the line.

"Um…" She gnawed her bottom lip. "He wanted to go for a walk, but then he got lost."

"Uh-huh." Hands on her hips, miles behind on the morning's lesson, Josie said, "Get in line. Bonnie, you, too."

Bonnie tilted her head back and screamed.

Not just your garden-variety kindergarten outrage, but a full-blown tantrum generally reserved for toy store emergencies. A whole minute later she was still screaming so loud that her classmates put their hands over their ears.

Josie tried reasoning with her, but Bonnie wouldn't hush longer than the few seconds it took to drag in a fresh batch of air. Not sure what else to do, Josie resorted to pressing the intercom's call button.

"Office."

"Cami!" Josie shouted over Bonnie, "I need Nat down here right away."

The door burst open and Shelby ran in. "What's wrong? Sounds like someone's dying."

Nat followed, out of breath and barely able to speak. "C-Cami said it sounds like someone's dying."

Both women eyed the squirming student lineup and then Bonnie. Betsy stood alongside her, whispering something only her twin could hear—that is, if she'd quieted enough to listen.

"Sweetie," Josie tried reasoning with the girl, "if Green Bean is your pet, I won't let him go, but we'll have to call your father to come get him. You know it's against our rules to bring pets to school when it's not for show-and-tell."

For Josie's ears only, Natalie said, "Hang tight, I'll get hold of her dad."

"Look," Dallas said an hour later. When he'd gotten the counselor's call, he'd been out on the back forty, vaccinating late summer calves. It was a wonder he'd even heard his cell ring. "If my girl said the snake got in her teacher's desk by accident, then that's what happened. Nobody saw her do it. Even if it did purposely end up there, how many boys are in her class? Could one of them have done it?" In the principal's office, Bonnie sat on one of his knees, Betsy on the other. Stroking their hair, he added, "I'm a busy man. I don't appreciate having to come all the way down here for something so minor."

Principal Moody sighed. With gray hair, gray suit and black pearls, she looked more like a prison guard than someone who dealt with children. "Mr. Buckhorn, in many ways schools are communities. Much like the town of Weed Gulch, our elementary maintains easy to understand *laws* by which all of our citizens must abide. I've been at this job for over thirty-five years and not once have I seen a snake *accidentally* find its way into a teacher's desk. I have, however, encountered fourteen cases of students placing their reptiles in various inappropriate locations."

Hardening his jaw, Dallas asked, "You calling my girl a liar? Look how upset she still is…"

Bonnie hiccupped and sniffled.

The woman rambled on. "All I'm suggesting is that Bonnie may need additional lessons on appropriate classroom behavior. Perhaps you and your girls should schedule a conference with Miss Griffin?"

Imagining the girls' scowling teacher, Dallas wondered what kind of crazy dust he'd snorted to have found her the least bit attractive. "As I'm sure you know, I went to this school, as did all of my brothers. My parents never had to deal with this kind of accusatory attitude."

"You're right," the principal said. "When y'all attended Weed Gulch Elementary, a simple paddling resolved most issues."

After ten more minutes of way-too-polite conversation that got him nowhere, Dallas hefted himself and his girls to their feet and said, "These two will be leaving now with me. Is there something I need to sign?"

The principal rose from her regal leather chair. "Miss Cami in the front office will be happy to show you the appropriate forms."

WITH EVERYONE BACK AT THEIR tables, chubby fingers struggling with the letter *F,* Josie sat at her desk multitasking. On a good day, she managed putting happy stickers on papers, entering completion grades on her computer and eating a tuna sandwich. On this day, she had accomplished only one out of three.

What sort of excuse would the twins' father make this time? He and the girls had been in the principal's office for nearly an hour.

"Missus *Gwiffin?*" She glanced up to find Charlie Elton sporting a broken crayon. He also had several missing teeth. "I *bwoke* it. *Sworry.*"

"It's okay, sweetie." Taking the red oversize crayon, she peeled off the paper from the two halves. "See? Now it works again."

"*Thwanks!*" All smiles, he dashed back to his table. Toothless grins were what led her to teaching. Feeling that every day she made a positive difference in her students' lives was what kept her in the career. Which was why the tension mounting between herself and the Buckhorn twins was so troubling. Not only was her job usually satisfying, but school was her haven.

This weekend, she'd head into Tulsa. There were some school specialty stores that might have classroom management books to help with this sort of thing.

The door opened and in shuffled the sources of her seemingly constant consternation.

"Hi," Josie said, wiping damp palms on her navy corduroy skirt. "Everything all right?"

"Daddy brought Green Bean's jar," Bonnie said with enough venom to take down a pit viper.

"He's got Green Bean and said we need to get our stuff and go home." Betsy looked less certain about their mission.

"Sure that's what you want to do?" Josie asked, kneeling in front of the pair. "We're learning about the letter *F.*"

"Let's stay," Betsy said in a loud whisper. "I *love* to color new letters."

Bonnie shook her head.

At the door, their father poked his head in. "Get a move on, ladies. I've still got work to do."

"Okay, Daddy." Hand in hand, the girls dashed to their cubbies.

"Mr. Buckhorn…" Josie rose, approaching him slowly in hope of attracting as few little onlookers as possible. Today, the stern set of his features made him imposing. Miles taller than he usually seemed. Yet something about the way he cradled Bonnie's pet in the crook of his arm gave him away as a closet teddy bear when it came to his girls. Trouble was, as a parent—or even a teacher—you couldn't be nice all the time. "While the twins gather their things, could we talk?"

He gestured for her to lead the way to the hall.

With the classroom door open, allowing her a full view of her diligently working students, Josie said, "I'm sorry this incident inconvenienced you. Pets are only allowed on certain days of the year."

"So I've heard." *Cold* didn't come close to describing the chill of his demeanor.

"Yes, you see, the snake itself is the least of our problems."

"*Our* problems?" He cocked his right eyebrow.

"Bonnie and Betsy—well, in this case mainly Bonnie, but—"

"Hold it right there." In her face, he whispered, "I'm sick and tired of accusations being made against my kids when their class is no doubt full of hooligans."

"Hooligans?" Maybe it was the old-fashioned word itself, or the sight of harmless Thomas Quinn wiping his perpetually runny nose on his sleeve—whatever had brought on a grin, she couldn't seem to stop.

"Think this is funny? We're talking about my daughters' education."

"I know," she said, sobering, trying not to notice how his warm breath smelled strangely inviting. Like oatmeal and cinnamon. "Mr. Buckhorn, I'm sorry. Really I am. I'm not sure how we've launched such a contentious relationship, but you have to know I only have the twins' best interests in mind. Kindergarten is the time for social adjustments. Nipping problem behaviors before they interfere with the real nuts and bolts of crucial reading and math skills."

"Why do you keep doing that? Implying my girls are difficult? Look at them," he said, glancing into the room where Bonnie and Betsy had gravitated to their assigned seats and sat quietly coloring with the rest of the class. "Tell me, have you ever seen a more heartwarming sight?"

Nope. Nor a more uncharacteristic one!

Typically by this time of day, Bonnie had carried out her second or third dastardly plan. Whether *freeing* the inhabitants of their ant farm or counting how many pencils fit in the water fountain's drain, the girl was always up to something. Betsy either provided cover or assisted in a speedy getaway.

"They're even self-starters," he boasted. "Their mother opened her own horse grooming shop. Looks to me like I have a couple of entrepreneurs on my hands."

"I agree," Josie was honestly able to say. The girls were already experts when it came to launching funny business. "But with all due respect, the twins are currently on their best behavior. With you here, I doubt they'll find trouble."

"Right. Because it's not them causing it in the first place."

Josie might as well have been talking to a rock wall. "My job is to make sure Bonnie and Betsy are prepared to do their best in first grade, right?"

He snorted. "Only correct thing you've said since I've been standing here."

"All right, then—" she propped her hands on her hips and glared "—what do I have to gain by making up outrageous stories about your girls?"

The question stumped him.

"That's right," she continued. "A big, fat nothing. No one wants the twins to be perfect more than me. Their future behavior is a reflection of not only your parenting, but my teaching."

"Why are you bringing me into this?" He switched Green Bean to the crook of his other arm.

Just when she thought she'd broken through the wall….

"I mentioned this to you before, but I really think it would help the situation," she said, recalling a child development class she'd had where parents sat behind two-way mirrors, watching the differences in their children's behavior once they'd left the room. "How about if starting tomorrow, you attend class with Bonnie and Betsy? Just for a few days."

It wouldn't be as idyllic as a blind study, but at least it would give her a stress-free week, plus maybe in some small way show the girls their father cared about their actions at school.

"Seriously?" He scratched his head. "What good is that going to do?"

In a perfect world, open your eyes to the scam your angels have been pulling.

AFTER DINNER, DALLAS MADE a beeline for the barn to muck stalls. He told himself it was because the horses deserved a perfectly clean environment, but the truth of the matter was that he needed time alone to think. As if listening to his mother lecture had been the price for heaping portions of her famous tuna casserole and peas, she'd yammered on and on about what pistols he and his brothers had been at school. And how she wasn't surprised to now find his proverbial apples not falling far from the tree.

Usually the scent of straw mingled with saddle leather and horseflesh soothed his darkest moods, but this one he found hard to shake. The principal's accusatory glare hadn't sat well. Yes, education was important, but it wasn't everything. After high school, some of Dallas's friends had gone on to college, but all he and Bobbie Jo had wanted was to get married and start their family. It didn't take a degree to learn ranching, but plenty of days spent working in brutal sun, cold and every sort of weather in between.

Lord, he missed his wife. She'd know what to do.

"Gonna be out here brooding all night?" His brother Wyatt broke the barn's peace. Wasn't there anywhere a man could go to be alone?

"I'm not brooding."

"Uh-huh." Tugging on leather gloves, Wyatt split a fresh hay bale in Thunder's stall.

The black quarter horse snorted his thanks.

"Just saw Mom. She told me to tell you the girls are waiting on you to read them a story and tuck them in."

"I know…" Wind whistled through the rafters, making the old building shudder.

"Then why aren't you with them?"

Dallas stabbed his pitchfork in the meager pile of dung he'd collected in the wheelbarrow. "Beats me."

"You gonna do it? Take the girls' teacher up on her offer?"

Glancing at his younger brother over his shoulder, Dallas asked, "Think I should?"

Wyatt hefted another bale, carrying it to the next stall. "I asked around and Josie Griffin is an excellent educator, not prone to spinning yarns. She's tough, yet compassionate. From what I've heard, always acting with her students' best interests at heart."

"Okay…so Miss Griffin's a saint. That doesn't mean she's justified in calling my girls trouble." Nor did it make him feel better about his wicked thoughts at the minigolf course.

"If that's truly the way you feel, then take her up on her offer. Henry and I will handle things around here." Henry was the ranch foreman and had been practically family since Dallas had been born.

"Not that simple," Dallas said, putting extra effort into cleaning Buttercup's stall. The palomino had been Bobbie Jo's. His wife had spent hours prepping to show the horse. Brushing her coat until Dallas could've sworn the mare purred. "What would you say if I told you there's a reason I don't want to be at that school?"

"What's more important than taking an active part in the twins' education?"

Dallas winced. Wyatt had always had a knack for zeroing in on the heart of any matter. "That's just it. The other night, when Bonnie and Betsy had that gaggle of girls over for a sleepover, we ran into Miss Griffin."

Sighing, he admitted, "The sight of her rear end in faded jeans just about fried my brain. Not good, seeing how the last thing I need is to be hot for teacher."

Chapter Three

Why wasn't Josie surprised Dallas had chosen to make a mockery of her suggestion?

Tuesday morning, on Weed Gulch Elementary's sun-drenched front lawn stood not one pony, but two. The docile pets put up with dozens of stroking little hands. For the students who weren't enraptured by cute creatures, there were cupcakes—dozens! Box after box of whimsically frosted treats, each sporting either plastic cowboy or cowgirl rings. In the center of the mayhem stood Dallas Buckhorn wearing jeans and a blue plaid Western shirt, accompanied by leather chaps, a Stetson hat and boots. Oh—the mere sight of him made her heart flutter, she'd give him that, but from a teaching standpoint, he'd ruined her whole day.

How was making construction paper analog clocks and then learning to read them going to top this?

"Miss Griffin!" Bonnie and Betsy ran up to her, hugging so hard around her waist that Josie nearly toppled over.

"Did you see what our daddy brought?"

"I sure did…" And we're going to have a nice, long talk about it. "Are those your ponies?"

"Uh-huh," Betsy said with a vigorous nod. "Mine is named Cookie because she has chocolate chip spots."

"Mine's Cinderella," Bonnie noted. "Just like the princess because she has long, blond hairs."

"Those are wonderful names." Josie was glad she'd worn capris and sneakers as the lawn she marched across was still dew-soaked. "You two were clever to match them so well to each pony."

"Thanks!" both girls said, skipping alongside her.

Before dashing ahead, Betsy shouted to her sister, "Come on, Cinderella pooped!"

Giggles abounded.

Thank goodness the older kids were already in class or off-color bathroom jokes would already be spreading. When it came to potty humor, fifth and sixth graders were experts.

"I've got a man here to clean all of this." Josie had been so focused on what she'd say to Dallas that she hadn't noticed he'd come up beside her.

Hand to her chest, she said, "You startled me."

"Sorry." Nodding toward the shrieking kids, he added, "I knew the ponies would be a hit, but I didn't expect a riot."

"When it comes to kindergartners, it doesn't take much."

"I'm seeing." His smile rocketed through her. Despite his many faults, he was undeniably handsome. Never more so than now. It was clear he belonged outside. The sun lightening his Buckhorn-blue eyes. Glancing over his shoulder, he signaled to an older man who knelt alongside Bonnie, helping her with her pet.

"Yeah, boss?" The man's easy smile, laugh lines at the corners of brown eyes and weathered skin had Josie guessing him to be in his mid-fifties. His playful spirit around the kids made him seem much younger. Like Dallas, he wore Western wear complete with a cowboy hat.

"Josie Griffin, meet Henry Pohl. He's worked our ranch longer than I've been alive."

Shaking Josie's hand, the man winked. "I wouldn't say it was *that* long. You are getting a tad long in the tooth."

In under twenty minutes, Dallas was true to his word and had begun loading the ponies into a custom, miniaturized horse trailer attached to a shiny black pick-up. The Buckhorn Ranch emblem of two battling rams had been stenciled on both doors.

While settling the children into their daily routine of standing for the Pledge of Allegiance, stilling for a moment of silence and then getting out their printing paper to practice writing their new letter and number, she watched Dallas through the wall of windows overlooking the school's front lawn.

Firmly, yet gently, he corralled the suddenly stubborn animals into their temporary home. With Henry's help, Dallas soon had all of the cupcake liners and white bakery boxes in the trash, leaving the area looking untouched save for sneaker tracks trailing through silvery dew.

Josie's students fidgeted and fussed. Too hyper from

cupcakes and fun to want to settle into their routine. The childlike part of her she didn't often let escape sympathized with them. Outside, it was shaping up to be a beautiful fall day. She had dreaded Dallas's visit, but was now surprised to be anticipating his return to the room.

"YOU DO KNOW YOUR CIRCUS broke about sixteen school rules?"

Dallas took another bite of his ham and swiss sandwich and shrugged. "Way I see it, my girls need to know I'm not here to punish them. I want them and their friends to be happy I'm in for a visit."

Josie Griffin pressed her full lips together like there was a whole lot she wanted to say, but was holding back.

"Out with it," he coaxed, biting into a pear. It was the first one he'd had in a while. Firm, yet juicy and sweet. Kind of like he'd imagine kissing Josie would be—that is, if she'd ever erase her pucker. Not that he'd done a whole lot of thinking about kissing the teacher, but cute as she was, he wouldn't have been normal if the notion hadn't at least crossed his mind.

For the twenty minutes while the kids were at recess, Josie had suggested they hang out in the teachers' lounge. The room was unremarkable save for a pleasantly efficient window air-conditioning unit and grown-up chairs. Dallas hadn't realized how many muscles in his back could possibly ache until he'd spent his morning pretzelled into munchkin chairs.

"Since you asked…" Her eyes narrowed. Was she fixing to yell at him again? "I didn't invite you here to throw a party, but observe your daughters in their daily setting. My hope is that they'll soon grow comfortable enough with you being in their surroundings to revert back to their usual naughty behavior."

"Whoa. What you're essentially saying is that you've set a trap you hope they spring?"

She at least had the good graces to flush. "I would hardly call a long acknowledged child psychiatry technique a trap. More like a tool. I can sit here telling you about the girls' sins until I run out of breath, but that still won't make you a believer. I want you to catch them in action. Only then will you understand how disruptive their pranks are to my class."

"And if they turn out to be the good kids I expect them to be?"

She damn near choked on a carrot stick. "Not that I'm a betting woman, but if I were, I'd put down a hundred on Bonnie and Betsy finding some form of trouble by the end of the day."

"You say that with such glee," he noted, wadding up his trash. "Like you want my daughters in hot water."

"Far from it. They need to understand that school is for learning, not horseplay. But wait—with this morning's stunt, you've pretty much blown that lesson out of the water."

"For the record—" he eased his legs out in front of him to cross at the ankles "—Cookie and Cinderella aren't horses, but ponies."

JOSIE WAS BEYOND MORTIFIED when Thursday morning had come and gone and still the twins hadn't so much as dropped a pencil shaving. Had she been wrong about them? Overexaggerated their penchant for mischief?

"Hungry?" Dallas asked as twenty-one squirming bodies raced for the door.

"I am," she said, motioning for the line leaders to guide them to the hand-washing station. "It's fried chicken day. Want to brave the cafeteria?"

"Is it safe?"

She laughed. "On turkey tetrazzini day," she wrinkled her nose, "not so much, but you're actually in for a treat. Mashed potatoes and white gravy with big yeast rolls. If we're really lucky, chocolate cake for dessert."

"I'm in." His white-toothed grin was made brighter by faint golden stubble. Not enough time to shave before beating the first bell?

After getting everyone through the line, Josie turned to Paula the lunch lady and said, "Please give Mr. Buckhorn a double serving and put it on my tab."

"Yes, ma'am." Heaping on gravy, the bosom-heavy brunette asked, "How's your cat? Heard he had a sick spell."

"Better, thanks." Josie loved how everyone in the school was an extended family. What she lacked for company at home, she more than made up for at work. "How's Teddy's job hunt?"

"Great." Her sixteen-year-old had been saving for a car. "He starts at the drive-in on Friday."

"Wonder—"

"I hate you, Thomas! Take your stupid cake!"

Josie peered through the serving-line door just in time to see Bonnie fling a chocolate square at poor little Thomas Quinn. As if that wasn't bad enough, she then smashed it into his hair.

"I hate you, too!" Betsy hollered. "Bonnie's a princess and you should've just given her the stupid cake."

"Girls, knock it off!" Dallas said, surging into the melee.

Thomas started to wail and showed no signs of letting up. "Sh-she g-got cake on my new g-glasses!"

"Let me clean those for you, bud." Dallas set his lunch tray on the table and then took the boy's gold-rimmed frames. To Josie, he said, "Be right back."

"Th-there's c-cake on my shirt, t-too. Mommy's gonna yell."

"No she won't, sweetie," Josie assured the boy. To the twins, she demanded, "What were you thinking?"

Hands on her hips, Bonnie said, "He should've just gave me that cake."

"Yeah," Betsy said, adopting the same pose.

"I'm Bonnie Buckhorn." Wearing a satisfied grin, Bonnie added, "Daddy says I'm one half of a perfect bunch and that I can do whatever I want."

After handing Thomas his freshly cleaned glasses, Dallas grabbed the collars of his daughters' matching pink T-shirts. "Ladies, we need to talk."

If Dallas hadn't seen the whole incident with his own eyes, he never would've believed it. Steering the girls into their quiet, dark classroom, he said, "Put your behinds in your chairs."

"But, Daddy," Bonnie whined, "why are we in trouble when Thomas was the one being mean?"

"We gave him cupcakes," Betsy thoughtfully pointed out.

Dallas rubbed his throbbing forehead. "You can't just take your friend's dessert. It's wrong. And—"

"You tell us we can do whatever we want." His eldest by a minute held his stare.

"Yes, but, hon, that doesn't give you the right to do bad things." Was everything else his girls had been accused of true?

"We aren't bad, Daddy." Betsy left her chair to crawl onto his lap. Bonnie soon followed.

"I'm sorry, Daddy." Bonnie wrapped her chubby arms around his neck.

"Both of you need to get it through your pretty heads that just because you're Daddy's princesses, that doesn't give you the right to do whatever you want. At school, you have to follow the rules."

Bonnie chimed in with, "Miss Griffin never said we couldn't put cake in Thomas's hair."

The statement was so ridiculous, Dallas had to chuckle. "Honey, I can think of very few situations where you *should* put cake in anyone's hair."

"Do you still love us?" Betsy asked.

Hunching over, he made growling, tickle monster noises, attacking their rib cages to the accompaniment of shrieking laughs.

Now that both girls had been scolded, it felt good to return to their usual Buckhorn family fun.

"WHO WANTS COFFEE AND DONUTS?" Friday morning, Josie halted her walk around the classroom to see Dallas and his girls wielding *snacks*.

"Me, me!" The majority of the class didn't even bother raising their hands before running over to claim their share.

Betsy and Bonnie beamed.

Thomas sank down in his chair.

"Stop!" Josie hated always being the bad guy, but this was ridiculous. "The school has a healthy snack policy and last I checked, coffee and donuts aren't on the list."

"But it's Friday," Dallas complained, sounding suspiciously like his daughters. "Plus," he nodded across the room, "as an apology, my girls wanted to give a special offering to that little fella."

If Thomas scooted much lower, he'd have dissolved into a puddle on the floor.

"I don't care if it's Christmas," Josie argued, "you're not caffeinating my kindergarteners."

"You're impossible." Turning his back on her, he said to his crew, "Come on, girls."

"Where are you going?" Josie asked, following them into the hall.

"Teachers' lounge. Or will you deny your coworkers a happy start to their weekend, too?"

Beyond furious with the man, she folded her arms and

watched them go. Unfortunately, back in the classroom, she was met with much whining and pouty stares.

Nipping that behavior, she refocused her students on their daily writing practice. When Bonnie and Betsy returned with their father, she already had their tablets and pencils ready to go.

"You're a killjoy," Dallas noted once she sat at her desk to finish writing next week's lesson plans.

"And you're a child disguised in a grown-up's body."

"A *man's* body," he said with the slow grin she'd grown to alternately hate and adore. Every time he pulled this stunt, he was usually trying to get himself out of hot water. No wonder his children were such a mess. Look who they had for an example! Worse yet, Dallas wielded that grin like a weapon. Same as his daughters, he knew how to pour on the charm.

"You're impossible."

"Thanks." He had the gall to combine his grin with a wink.

How, she didn't know, but Josie managed to survive the morning and lunch hour and even afternoon recess without suffering a meltdown. Everywhere she went there was Dallas, being generally helpful and offering to pass out papers. Which only put her that much more on edge.

Friday afternoons, she always introduced an art project that was fun, but also worked on building a sense of community. For this week's lesson, she'd had the children draw names of a friend. Once paired up, they would then create each other's portraits with finger paint.

After letting each student pick a cover-up from the pile of men's and women's oxford shirts she'd collected at yard sales, she passed out the oversize paper and spent a few minutes going over ground rules.

"Now," she asked once she'd finished, "raise your hand if you can tell me where the paint goes."

Megan Brown was first. "On the paper!"

"Right. Excellent." Over the years, Josie had learned to never underestimate the importance of explaining this point. "Does anyone have questions?"

Thomas raised his hand. "I forgot how to get the lids off the jar thingees."

"Like this," Josie said, holding up a plastic container from the nearest table. "Just twist, and then carefully set your lid on the table. Stick your hand in one finger at a time to get your paint. Kind of like your finger is the brush. Make sense?"

He pushed up his glasses and nodded.

"Any other questions? Okay, let's take the lids off our containers and begin."

Since the twins were on opposite sides of the room, Dallas spent a few minutes with one before moving on to the other. When he was with Betsy, Josie happened to be alongside him. "My girl's pretty talented, huh?"

"A future Picasso," Josie said in all seriousness. Betsy had indeed captured her friend Julia's essence in a primary colored abstract extravaganza.

"Their mom was pretty talented."

Looking up at her dad, Betsy asked, "What'd Mommy make?"

A wistful look settled on his usually stoic features.

It softened him. Gave him a vulnerability Josie hadn't before noticed. "She used to set up her easel and water-colors by the duck pond and paint for hours. I teased her that her long hair rode the breeze like weeping willow branches."

The warmth in his eyes for a woman long gone knotted Josie's throat.

"Sometimes she'd paint what she saw." He tweaked his daughter's nose. "Other times, especially when she was pregnant with you, she'd paint what she imagined. Like one day sharing a picnic with you and your sister."

"Sounds amazing," Josie said. "I've always wanted to be more artistic."

Upon hearing her voice, Dallas suffered a barely perceivable lurch—as if until she'd spoken, he'd forgotten anyone but he and Betsy were even in the room.

"Yeah, well…" He cleared his throat. Did he even know what she'd said?

"Stop, Bonnie!" Megan began crying. "I don't wanna get in trouble for you!"

Josie's stomach sank. So much for her peaceful afternoon.

"What happened?" she asked upon facing a horrible mess of what she presumed was Bonnie's making. Her entire paper was coated with paint, as well as the table and carpeting underneath.

"Well…" Bonnie planted her paint-covered fists on her shirt. "Since Megan is tall, I ran out of paper. I tried getting you, but you were talking to Daddy. I didn't have anywhere else to paint, so I painted the floor."

The girl stated her actions in such a matter-of-fact way that they nearly sounded plausible. Nearly.

Don't yell. Keep your composure.

"Bonnie," Josie said after forcing a few nice deep breaths, "just because you ran out of paper, that doesn't give you the right to complete your project wherever you'd like."

"You're not the boss of me," the girl sassed. "My daddy is, and he—"

Dallas stepped up behind her. "—would like you to follow him to the cleanup closet where you'll get a bucket and sponge to clean *your* mess."

Looking at her father as if he'd spouted bull horns, Bonnie's mouth gaped. "But—"

"Move it," Dallas said, not even trying to hide his angry tone.

An hour later, Josie had gotten everyone tidied and on their way home for the weekend. Back in the classroom, Betsy sat cross-legged on a dry patch of carpet. Dallas had found a roll of brown paper towels and sopped the areas where Bonnie had scrubbed.

On her way inside from putting her students on buses, Josie had stopped by the janitor's office and he'd assured her that his steam cleaner would tackle the job. By Monday morning, no one would ever guess the vandalism had taken place. Josie hated thinking of a small child's actions in such harsh terms, but Bonnie had known exactly what she'd been doing.

"Almost done?" Josie asked.

"Uh-huh." Bonnie looked exhausted, but that hardly excused her from the consequences of her actions.

According to the classroom discipline chart, this was a major offense. Punishable by missing the next week's recesses.

"Miss Griffin?" Betsy asked. "If we buy you a present, can you stop hating us?"

"Why would you think I hate you?" Josie asked, hurt by the very notion.

"Because you always look at us with a frowning face."

The knot returned to Josie's throat, only this time for a different reason. The Buckhorn family packed quite the emotional punch. "I'm not making a mad expression, sweetie, but sad. When my students break rules on purpose, it makes me feel like I'm not a very good teacher or you would've known better."

"I guess." Tracing the carpet's blue checkered pattern, the girl didn't sound convinced.

Dallas took his wallet from his back pocket. "Clearly, Bonnie and I are not going to be able to make this right without a shop vacuum. If I give you a couple hundred, think that'll cover the cost of getting someone out here to clean?"

"This isn't about money," Josie said, saddened that he'd even asked. "The custodian will handle whatever you can't get up. But, Bonnie, what lesson have you learned?"

The little girl released a big sigh. "I learned if I paint the floor, I don't wanna get caught."

Chapter Four

"Wrong," Dallas snapped. Bonnie's bratty answer made him sick to his stomach. It reminded him of the epic battles his parents and younger sister, Daisy, had had when she was a kid. When she'd taken off right after her high school graduation, Georgina and Duke blamed themselves for not having used a stronger hand in dealing with her many antics. Now, with the benefit of hindsight, he understood his parents' pain over their own failings. Damn, he hated being wrong, and when it came to his daughters' poor behavior, not only had his mother been right, but their teacher had been, too. As a parent, he looked like a fool and had no one to blame but himself. "The lesson you were supposed to have learned was that if you'd followed Miss Griffin's directions, you wouldn't now be in trouble."

Bonnie put her hands over her ears and stomped her feet. "You said I'm a princess and that means I only do what I want!"

"Clearly," he said to Josie, too embarrassed to meet her gaze, "Bonnie and I are failing to communicate."

"That's okay," Betsy said while her sister screamed.

"Bonnie does this to me when I tell her to share Barbie's clothes."

"How do you get her to stop?" Josie asked.

"Tell her if she doesn't stop, I'm going to tell Nanny Stella."

Great plan, but the middle-aged woman who'd cared for the twins practically since the day they'd been born just happened to have quit.

Grimacing, he scooped up his little hellion, tossing her over his shoulder. "Miss Griffin," he managed over Bonnie's increased volume, "I'm not exactly sure how, but by Monday, I promise to have this situation under control."

Betsy rolled her eyes.

By the time Dallas turned his truck onto the dirt road leading home, Bonnie was asleep and Betsy huffed on her window with her breath, drawing stars and hearts in the fog.

He wouldn't have blamed Josie Griffin if she'd laughed him out of the school. Bonnie's behavior had been unacceptable. How had she managed to get so spoiled without him noticing?

At the memory of how many times his mother or one of his brothers or Josie had warned him of impending doom, heat crept up his neck and cheeks. How had Bonnie gotten to this point? He gave her everything she'd ever wanted. What was he missing?

Dallas knew his mother was the logical person to turn to for advice, but he also knew her sage counsel came at a price—admitting he'd been wrong. Only his shame wouldn't end there. She'd delight in telling his brothers and sister-in-law, neighbors and old family friends just what a disaster he was as a father. Give her twenty-four hours and she'd have blabbed his predicament to everyone between Weed Gulch and the Texas border.

Unacceptable.

Tightening his grip on the wheel, he turned onto the ranch's drive. His brother Wyatt didn't have kids, meaning he didn't know squat about rearing them. Cash and his wife, Wren, had one-year-old Robin, but that cutie could barely walk, let alone sass.

Which left only one option—Josie Griffin.

Not only was the woman highly trained on the inner workings of the kindergarten mind, but by not rubbing his face in his failings, she'd made him feel less of a fool. She could've laughed at him during Bonnie's fit. Instead, she'd quietly and efficiently gathered his girls' things and the cowboy hat he'd hung from the coat pegs at the back of the room, delivering them all the way out to his truck.

At the ranch, Dallas carried Sleeping Beauty into the house, laying her on the sofa. While Betsy tucked a pillow under her head, he took the throw blanket from his favorite chair, draping it over his girl.

"She all right?" his mother asked, wiping her hands on a dishrag on her way into the room. "That child *never* sleeps this early in the day."

Betsy was all too happy to volunteer, "Bonnie got in *big* trouble at school."

"Oh?" Dallas's mother sat on the sofa arm, smoothing Bonnie's blond hair. "What happened?"

"Well…" Hands on her hips, Betsy sported a huge smile. "First, she—"

"Can it, squirt." Dallas could feel a headache coming on. "Go clean your room."

"No." Arms folded, chin raised, Betsy retorted, "If Bonnie gets to sleep, I don't wanna work."

Teeth clenched, Dallas silently counted to five. What was going on around here? He'd never had the slightest problem with either of his girls—especially not Betsy—now, she was also giving him lip?

"Betsy," his mother warned. "Do as your father asked. Your dirty clothes need to be in the hamper."

"Yes, ma'am." Chin to her chest, Betsy pouted on her way toward the stairs.

"Honey," his mother said, her tone characteristic of a nice, long speech, "you know I don't usually interfere with your personal business, but—"

Dallas snorted. "With all due respect, save it. After the day I've had, I'm seriously not in the mood." Taking his keys and wallet from the entry-hall table, he asked, "Need anything from the store? I'm going to town."

"Why? You just came from the girls' school. I don't understand why you'd now be driving all the way back, when—"

"Dogs on a biscuit, Mama, could you just this once leave me alone?"

Shaking her head, she snapped, "I'll leave you alone when you agree to get your head out of your behind."

"KITTY, GIMME A BREAK. Thanks to the Trouble Twins, I'm only twenty minutes late." Judging by her cat's frantic meows, he'd had a long, hard day lounging on his window seat in the sun.

Josie set her purse, keys and mail on the kitchen table, abandoning her plan to glance through a Victoria's Secret sale catalog. After taking a can of Filet Mignon Surprise from the cabinet, she popped off the top and spooned it onto a saucer. Kitty not only liked fine food, but eating it on fine bone china.

"You do know you're spoiled rotten," Josie noted as she set the cat's dinner on the floor. Considering how she catered to her "baby," was it fair for her to think of Dallas as being such an awful parent?

Had Emma lived, would I be any better?

Sighing, she took an oatmeal scotchie from the cookie jar, then lost herself in making imaginary purchases.

Fifteen minutes later, her phone rang. One glance at the caller ID and her stomach lurched. "Hello?"

"Josie, this is Dallas. Hope you don't mind me calling after hours, but your number was in the book, so I figured—"

"It's fine," she assured him, kneeling to pick up the cat's empty dish. "Is something wrong with the girls?"

"Not exactly. More like me."

"Oh?" Dish in the sink, she wasn't sure what else to say. "I'm sorry. Is there anything I can do to help?"

"Yeah, well…" He cleared his throat. "What I was hoping is that if you aren't too busy, you could meet me at Lucky's for a quick coffee. I'd only need a few minutes of your time. This wouldn't be like a date—just me picking your brain for kid management ideas."

A smile played across her lips. How the great Dallas Buckhorn had fallen after considering himself World's Finest Father. "You're welcome to more than a few minutes. Maybe even sixty."

"Really?" His tone grew brighter. "That'd be great. How soon can you be here?"

"You mean you want me to meet you now?" Not that she had anything special on tap for her Friday night other than a load of laundry.

"That was kind of my plan—that is, if you're amenable."

"Sure," she said, telling herself her pulse had become erratic from pacing rather than thoughts of sharing an intimate booth with the man with no distractions other than an occasional waitress refilling their drinks. It was tough enough keeping her cool around him in front of her class. On her own? Whew. "Um, I suppose I could fit you into my schedule."

"Oh, hell. I forgot it's the weekend. Do you already have plans?" He actually sounded as nervous as she felt.

"No," she said, reminding herself that, like the man had told her, this was hardly a date. More like an off-campus parent/teacher conference. As such, there was no logical explanation for why she'd taken the cordless phone into her walk-in closet, already searching for the right thing to wear. "Give me a few minutes to change out of my school clothes and I'll be right over."

DALLAS STOOD WHEN JOSIE approached.

She'd ditched her simple work dress in favor of jeans,

a tight black T-shirt and those red boots of hers he'd already decided he liked. Her hair hung long and loose and wild. He liked that, too. He tried not to notice how her curls framed her full breasts.

"Sorry," she said, hustling between tables to get to his booth. "I'd have been here sooner, but got held up by a train."

"Hazard of small-town living."

Sliding onto her black vinyl seat, she laughed. "True."

"Hungry? The coconut cream pie is great."

She wrinkled her nose. "Thanks, but I'm not a big fan of coconut. Had an incident as a child. Long story."

"Fair enough." Had her smile always been so contagious? "Blueberry á la mode?"

"Now, *that,* I can do. With a hot tea, please."

He signaled to the waitress and gave her their order.

With pleasantries out of the way, Dallas was unsure of his next move. Issues with his girls that'd seemed pressing back at the ranch now felt embarrassing.

"It's okay, you know."

"What?" He looked up to find her staring. Smiling. Unwittingly making his chest tight with the kind of attraction he hadn't felt for a woman in God only knew how many years.

"For you to ask for help with Bonnie and Betsy. They'll turn out fine. You just need to set boundaries now as opposed to when they're sixteen and drag racing their matching Lamborghinis."

With a grimace, he said, "Guess I deserve that."

Reaching across the table, she covered his hands with hers. Not only was her gesture comforting, but joltingly erotic. As if her fingertips were supercharged with emotion and heat. "Promise, I was only teasing. And please, don't take this the wrong way, but in my professional opinion, you've equated loving your girls with letting them have or do whatever they want."

Nodding, he admitted, "My mom says the same thing. But for the life of me, I can't see why making my girls happy is wrong." More important, he'd promised Bobbie Jo that no matter what, their children would always be his top priority.

"It's not wrong. It's wonderful. But part of making them well-rounded people is teaching them self-discipline and to follow rules and routines. Right now, Bonnie and Betsy seem to struggle in those areas. All I'm suggesting is that you start with baby steps to establish a sort of baseline order."

"Okay, whoa…" Dallas whooshed his hand over his head. "You lost me back at routines."

"Take, for instance, their school routines. In order to get my students used to their new classroom setting as opposed to hanging out at home, where their days are less structured, we do the same things over and over until they become second nature. We make lines for hand washing and recess and lunch. We say the pledge and then first thing every morning review our previous days' letters and learn a new one. Because our schedule rarely varies—unless some parent shows up with cupcakes and ponies—" she winked "—by the end of the first quarter, most of my little munchkins could probably tell a substitute what they should be covering at any given time."

For the life of him, Dallas failed to see what all that had to do with him. "As far as routines—tooth brushing and bath and bedtimes and stuff—that's all Nanny Stella's domain."

"Who makes sure they do their homework?"

"Used to be Nanny Stella. Now…" He shrugged.

"And chores?"

Starting to get the picture, Dallas reddened.

"Enforcing table manners?"

"My mom, but if the girls are way out of line in playing with their food, I'll growl in their direction."

Josie frowned.

"What? Dad always ran a tight ship when it came to mealtimes."

"Uh-huh. So let's see, pretty much the only interaction you have with the girls is at mealtime?"

"Not at all. We fish and go toy shopping and watch movies. They're all the time out in the barn with me, and a few days each week we pack a picnic and take off on trail rides."

"All of that sounds amazing but, Dallas, during any of that fun, do you ever get to be a disciplinarian?"

Luckily, he was spared answering Josie's latest question by the arrival of the pie and her tea.

The bell over the door jingled as a family of five came in for early supper. With yellow walls, faded linoleum floors and mismatched booths, the diner might have been lacking in decor, but the food was stick-to-your-ribs good. A couple soon entered, followed by another family. Why, Dallas couldn't say, but it made him feel good to see the empty diner filling. There was safety in numbers, and even though he'd asked Josie for help, he felt under attack. Which was ridiculous. His girls loved him and for now, that was enough.

"That was delicious," Josie said, patting her napkin to her lips. "I can't remember the last time I had pie."

"Mom makes it at least once a month."

Pouring herself a second cup of tea, she asked, "Do you ever get tired of living with your mom?"

"Surprisingly not. We get on each other's nerves, but since she lost Dad and I lost Bobbie Jo, we've leaned on each other."

"Makes sense," she said, swirling honey into her mug.

"How about you? After your husband died, who'd you turn to for support?"

Turning introspective, she said, "Mostly friends. My parents retired to Maine."

He whistled. "That's a long haul."

"No kidding."

"What moved them up there?"

She looked away. "Long story."

"I have time." He finished the last of his meringue.

"Wish I did." She grimaced while pushing herself out of the booth. "I don't know what I was thinking. I have an appointment."

He checked his watch. "It's nearly seven."

She flashed a hesitant smile, and not that he was by any means an expert when it came to deciphering women, but damned if she didn't look ready to cry. "I really should go."

An apology rode the tip of his tongue, but seeing how she already had one foot out the diner's door, it wouldn't do him a hell of a lot of good. Which led him to the conclusion that he'd have had a more productive evening staying in the barn to oil his saddle.

HALFWAY HOME, JOSIE SWIPED tears from her cheeks, feeling weak and silly. It'd been four years. Why had such a casual question concerning her parents caused a meltdown?

Maybe because with all of Dallas's talk about family, she knew she was a fraud? Oh, sure, when it came to deciphering the mind of a kindergartener, she was a pro, but when it came to her own damaged psyche, all bets were off.

In the house, Kitty hopped down from his window seat to rub against Josie's calves. She set her purse and keys on the entry-hall bench before picking up the cat, burying her face in his fur. "Why am I such a mess?"

Kitty answered with a satisfied purr.

Sighing, she returned Kitty to his favorite spot. Though she knew better than to make her next move, she did it anyway. One of her favorite features of her home was the split levels. The sunken living room. The three steps at the end of the hall leading to Emma's room.

Pushing open the door, greeted by the soft haze of sun setting beyond western-facing windows, she saw three-year-old Emma jumping on her canopy bed.

Giggling while building a block tower only to knock it down. Sleeping with lashes so long they'd brushed her cheeks.

Josie hugged herself, stepping farther into the room. Deeper into her daughter's spell. Her parents had begged her to change the sanctuary into a sewing or exercise room. To reclaim the space for herself. What they didn't understand was that touching Emma's bird nest collection, gathered from nature hikes and from the yard after storms, if only for a moment, returned Josie's daughter to her arms. Upon finding each treasure, she'd said a singsong prayer for the winged creatures who'd lost their home before reverently handing it to her mother to be placed upon her "special" shelf. Then, Emma held out her arms to be picked up, asking Josie to tell her a story about all of the songbirds living in their backyard.

Together, they'd squeezed into the comfy armchair in Emma's room where Josie would spin tales of a fanciful bird kingdom presided over by bossy King Jay.

Seated in the chair, Josie ran her hands along the floral chintz upholstery, hoping to release some of her daughter's precious smell, knowing the action was futile, yet going through the motions all the same.

She hadn't indulged in licking her emotional wounds in a long time. Months. Maybe even a year. Yes, she'd been in the room to dust picture books and dolls, but not to mourn. More to celebrate the miracle her precious little girl had been.

The fact that she'd now backslid into the wreck she'd once been told her she wasn't anywhere near ready to be with another man—even for an outing as seemingly innocuous as talking over pie. Conversations naturally led to questions. The answers to which, she was too mortified to tell.

Chapter Five

Monday morning, though typically Nanny Stella would take the twins to school, Dallas volunteered for the chore. He told himself he wanted to spend more time with his girls, but truth be told, he was still irked by the way Josie had ditched him.

Yes, he might be attracted to her physically, but that only meant he was a man and all that that implied. After stewing on the issue all weekend, Dallas was ready for answers.

What he wasn't prepared for was finding Josie surrounded by three other teachers, looking red-eyed and blotchy as if she'd recently cried.

"What's wrong with Miss Griffin?" Bonnie asked. "She looks bad."

"Be nice," Dallas snapped, not in the mood for a repeat of his daughter's Friday performance.

"She was being nice, Daddy." Betsy raised her chin while grabbing her sister's hand. "Miss Griffin *does* look bad."

He shook his head. "Less talk and more stowing your gear."

"You mean our backpacks?" Bonnie scrunched her face. "'Cause I'm pretty sure I don't have anything called *gear*."

Upon steering his daughters toward their cubbies, Dallas helped remove lunches and Hello Kitty crayon boxes. Next on the agenda was making sure Green Bean had stayed home in his jar. Satisfied no immediate shenanigans were planned, he got both girls settled at their respective tables with their chubby pencils and writing tablets.

Satisfied both of his daughters were working as opposed to faking it until he turned his back, he went out into the hall.

Josie was finally on her own, greeting students as they entered her room.

"About Friday night…"

"Good morning, Thomas. Have a nice weekend?"

"Uh-huh," the boy said with an exaggerated nod. "We went to the Tulsa state fair and saw a *gigantimous* pumpkin the size of my dad's truck!"

With plans to go Wednesday night, the monster pumpkin was at the top of Dallas's girls' to-do list.

"Whoa," Josie said to her student without missing a beat. "That must've been amazing. Did you bring me a fried Twinkie?"

"Nooo!" he said with a giggle. "Mom said those cost, like, a million trillion dollars and we're not rich."

"Me, neither." Loudly sighing, she shook her head and smiled. "But when I win the lottery we'll go nuts. Buy all the fried food our stomachs can hold."

"Promise?"

Nodding, she rubbed the top of his head before pushing him into the room. "But before we start eating, you need to get to work on your review letters."

"Okay…" Head drooped, he marched off to put away his things.

Suddenly alone with Josie, Dallas found himself in the unfamiliar position of feeling like a five-year-old, vying for teacher's attention. "Where were we?"

Her smile pinched, she said, "Not sure, but regardless, I've got a long day ahead of me."

"I know—" he moved between her and the door "—and I'm sorry to barge in like this, but please, just tell me what I did to make you run off like that."

"Dallas…" The way she glanced at the ceiling and then back into her room, even the first grader skipping down the hall while playing with his zipper would've been smart enough to recognize Josie was trying to avoid him.

"I'm sorry. Whatever it was."

"No." Eyes pooling, she swallowed hard. "It's me who should be apologizing." Hand on his forearm, she managed, "I do need to get to my class, but—"

"If that's the case—you being in the wrong—make it up to me by going with Betsy, Bonnie and I to the state fair Wednesday night."

"I couldn't," she said. "I'm sure the girls have been looking forward to it and the last thing they'd want would be for their teacher tagging along."

Clearing his throat, Dallas reminded her, "Weren't you just telling me how I should be the grown-up? I want you to come. Plus, what better place for you to show me how to be the best possible dad."

"Dallas, thank you, but no." Edging around him, she'd almost made it through her door, only all of his work with calf wrangling had finally paid off in that he was a fraction of a second faster.

"Wrong answer. Agree to help me or when the girls show up for school on Thursday, they'll be so hopped up on cotton candy and caramel apples it may take you the rest of the week to get them off the ceiling."

She might've crossed her arms, but her frown showed signs of cracking.

"Worse yet," he persisted, "with me in charge, they might run wild, letting loose all of the livestock and pitching gum at all of the rides. It could damn well turn into an international incident."

Rolling her eyes, laughing but somehow not looking happy, she finally relented. "Okay, I'll go. But only because at this point, you sound as if you need more help than your girls."

"How are you?" Natalie asked the Wednesday afternoon before the fair, during their biweekly spa pedicures and manicures. The Korean family who ran the place spoke just enough English to do business, making it the perfect place for indulging in nice, long talks. "And I don't mean your polite version."

"Not going to lie…" Josie winced while her calluses were pumiced. "It was a rough weekend. Everything I did brought back painful memories of Emma."

"You should've called me." Natalie lightly rubbed Josie's forearm.

"I know, but I should be over it, you know? I don't mean forgetting my daughter, but at least being able to cope."

"What do you think brought this on?"

"No thinking involved. I can pinpoint the exact second it started. You know the disaster Friday turned out to be with the Trouble Twins, right?"

"Yes…" Nat grimaced.

"Well, out of the blue Friday night, Dallas called. Wanted me to meet him at the diner for coffee."

"Dallas Buckhorn? As in the most gorgeous man on the planet?" her friend interjected.

Josie laughed. "He's not *that* good-looking. And, anyway, would you just let me finish my story?"

"For the record—yes, he *is* that gorgeous. Though his brother Cash inches him out for the world title by a fraction, but please, do continue."

Loving her friend for making her laugh, Josie hit the high points of what'd happened, closing with, "All of his parenting questions made me think about Emma's silly tantrums and then about Hugh, and when Dallas asked why my parents were so far away in Maine, I lost it." Hands over her face, Josie forced a few deep breaths. "I hardly know the man. The last thing I wanted to share with him was how devastating it is to me that my own parents—people I thought were in my corner—moved half a continent away to avoid me."

"That's so not true. Your mom's geographically closer

to your brother and his wife and kids. They begged you to go."

Meeting her friend's gaze, Josie's mind flashed on her daughter's grave in the Weed Gulch cemetery. "You and I both know I'm not going anywhere."

"Josie…"

"Don't start on me."

"I'm not. Promise. I only wish you'd—"

"What *cullah?*" her nail technician asked.

Josie handed her a bottle of OPI's Candy Apple Red. To her friend, she said, "Did I mention Dallas asked me to go with him and his girls to the fair?"

"No, but I'm liking the sound of that. Getting right back on the dating horse. Good girl."

"It's hardly a date. The man needs my help and for my sanity, I need Bonnie and Betsy to chill."

"I WANT THAT GORILLA NOW!" Betsy punctuated her demand with a scream loud enough to make several passersby cover their ears while still others looked on not sure whether to call police.

"She *really* wants that gorilla, Dad." Bonnie, looking like a pint-size forty-year-old, calmly met his gaze.

"I'll try again," Dallas mumbled in front of a carnie's milk bottle game. "But I'm pretty sure these things are weighted."

"Daddy, I want it!" Betsy screamed.

Josie cleared her throat. "Not to butt into your business, but this would be a perfect time to drag Betsy away from here, explaining why she can't always have her way."

"You think?" Eyebrows raised, the man honestly appeared stunned by her suggestion. "She *really* wants it."

"I'd love a new Lexus, but that doesn't mean I'm getting one any time soon." Kneeling in front of the child, Josie took hold of her flailing hands. "Betsy, hon, I know the gorilla is pretty cool, but we're going to go look at some real animals. I heard there's a baby giraffe in the petting zoo."

"Gorillas are waaay better." Bonnie shoved a wad of cotton candy into her mouth.

"I—" sniffle "—still—" sniffle "—want—" sniffle "—him."

"Listen up, princess." Dallas hefted the girl into his arms. "Miss Josie is right. Let's head over to the real animals. If you're good, we'll get snow cones."

"O-okay."

While Dallas's new promise at least provided temporary calm, throbbing rock from the midway combined with temperatures in the muggy high-eighties proved not a good combination when Josie was already worn out from a tough day at school.

The petting zoo was more quiet, but also more frenzied with dozens of little bodies darting in all directions.

"Want to find an out-of-the-way bench?" Dallas asked.

"Sounds perfect."

While Josie found a seat, Dallas purchased feed for the girls, instructing them to stay within the fenced area.

"Feels good to take a load off," he said, gazing toward

his daughters who giggled while tiny goats nuzzled grain pellets from their palms. "Ready?"

"For what?" she asked with a sideways glance, trying to ignore tingly awareness on the side of her body where their thighs and shoulders brushed. She'd forgotten his size. How just being around him filled her with the sense that whatever happened—aside from kid disasters—he'd be in control.

"To tell me what was wrong Friday night?"

Her stomach sank. "Why do you care?"

"You're spending all of this time helping me with the twins, yet aside from buying you a half-dozen fried Twinkies, I've done nothing for you."

"First, I only had two Twinkies, thank you very much. Second, what's bugging me has nothing to do with you." Looking at her fresh manicure, she traced the outline of her cuticle. Maybe if she tried hard enough to avoid Dallas's probing gaze, he'd get the hint that she didn't want to share certain portions of her personal life.

"Sure? Because it wouldn't be the first time I ticked a woman off. The few times my mom's book club have tried fixing me up on blind dates they've ended in disaster."

Who wouldn't like you? was the first thing that entered her mind. Beyond his looks, Dallas was funny and hardworking and well-mannered. Had she been remotely interested in giving the whole relationship game another try, he would certainly be a prime candidate. But her last weeks with Hugh had been a nightmare. He'd singlehandedly taken everything she thought she'd known about love and turned it upside down.

"Once, ten minutes into our date, I asked a woman if her hair hurt."

"Why would you do that?" The question provided the perfect opportunity to angle away from him, giving herself space to breathe. Even over the barn's perfume of straw and manure, Dallas smelled of leather and citrus and sun. Like the kinds of outdoor adventures she'd never take.

"Evelyn had it all stacked up high with a bird wing barrette sticking out of the side. Looked like it was stabbing her. I thought I was being polite. Judging by her sudden need to stay home to clean carpets, she thought different."

"You're terrible," she admonished. "Kind of like a certain pair of your offspring…" Pointing toward a llama, Josie was already on her feet to hopefully ward off trouble.

Bonnie had climbed halfway over the fence, with Betsy not far behind. They'd dumped their feed buckets and now wore them as hats.

"Let me handle this," Dallas said, passing Josie midway.

Already out of breath, she paused, hunched over, bracing her hands on her knees.

Wonder of wonders, Dallas snagged each girl around their waist, giving them stony looks before setting them to their feet. "What are you two thinking?"

"Betsy wanted to kiss the llama," Bonnie explained, "but he wouldn't come close enough, so I was gonna try picking him up, but then I got stuck so Betsy was gonna help."

Hands braced on his hips, Josie was pleased to see Dallas finally looking the part of an aggravated father. "Not only could you both have been hurt, but what if you'd landed on top of the poor llama? Why do you think the fence is even there?"

"Just to bug us?" Betsy suggested. "It would've been lots easier to kiss him if there wasn't any fence."

"Yeah," Bonnie said. "That's my answer, too."

"You two are a mess." Dallas looked to the sky. "No wonder Miss Josie's tired of trying to fix your impossible behavior."

"That's not nice." Betsy's big blue eyes looked near tears. Directing her pouty look toward her teacher, she asked, "Do you hate us?"

"Of course, I don't hate you," Josie assured. "But your dad's right. I am tired of always scolding you. You're big girls. Too big to even think about going someplace you know you're not supposed to be."

"But—"

"Stop," Dallas said to Bonnie. "You're not going to talk your way out of this." Taking each girl by their hands, he led them toward the exit.

"You're going too fast!" Betsy complained.

"Should've thought about that before you tried breaking *into* a cage."

"Are we going to ride the Ferris wheel now?" The closer they got to the midway, the more excited Bonnie looked. "I love riding rides. It's the best."

Much to Josie's surprise—and delight—Dallas marched right past the Tilt-A-Whirl with its pulsing rock music. He did the same with fifteen other rides.

"Daddy, we're missing all of the good stuff." Betsy looked longingly toward the fun house.

"Uh-huh." On and on Dallas walked until finally stopping at his truck.

"Are we going to the *auntie em* to get more money to buy us more stuff?" Assuming this must be the case, she jumped up and down with excitement.

Betsy joined in on the celebration.

As the girls scrambled into the backseat of the extended cab, fastening their safety belts, Josie asked Dallas under her breath, "Where are we really going?"

"Home."

Josie flashed him a surreptitious thumbs-up.

Considering the twins' numerous tantrums followed by the attempted llama raid, enough was enough. Punishments were in order.

"There's an *auntie em*, Daddy." Bonnie pointed at a bank. "Get *lots* of money. I want a gorilla and more cotton candy and some of those purses."

"I want cheesecake on a stick!" Betsy bounced on her seat.

"Surprise," Dallas said, glancing in the rearview as he steered the truck off Yale Drive and onto westbound I44, "the only place you two are going is Choreville."

"Where's that, Daddy?" Bonnie had so much cotton candy in her mouth Josie was surprised she could even speak. "Is there lots of money?"

"Not likely." He passed a painfully slow minivan. "Since you'll be mucking out the horse stalls."

"What? Why?" Bonnie pitched her cotton candy bag

into the front seat. "I thought we were going back to the fair?"

"Nope."

From the backseat, tears and wails erupted. Wails so loud Josie had to fight the urge to cover her ears.

"Sorry about this," Dallas said.

"Me, too. I was looking forward to riding the mini-coaster."

His sideways glance and smile made her heart flutter. He'd always been handsome, but in light of his stern reaction to the fence-climbing incident, her new respect for him was infinitely more appealing than his rugged cowboy face. "Rain check for tomorrow night—this time, without squawking kiddos?"

"I can't," she said with genuine regret above continued backseat sobs, "I have a dance class."

"Seriously?"

"You say that like you can't imagine me performing even the most simple pirouette." Did she really come off as that clumsy?

"I didn't intend it like that— Cut it out back there. I can't hear myself think."

"You're mean!" Bonnie informed her father.

"Like I was saying," Dallas continued without acknowledging his child's latest complaint, "that came out wrong. Actually, I meant *seriously*, as in I'm impressed."

"Oh." Oddly enough, she'd wanted to be upset with him. It would have made it easier to tell herself she wasn't disappointed about missing out on a private night together.

"How about Friday?"

"I can go to the fair *any* night, Daddy." Suddenly tear-free, Betsy was all smiles.

"You're not invited," he noted. To Josie, he asked, "So? Up for a do-over?" His easy smile not only stole her breath, but crept into her long frozen heart.

Though she knew better, Josie said, "Absolutely."

Chapter Six

"When I asked you to join me on this thing, I didn't plan on staying up here the whole night." Dallas peered over the edge of the Ferris wheel's car, more than a little queasy about how small all of the people looked below.

"I think it's kind of cool." Far from being spooked by the height, Josie gazed at the panoramic view with enough wide-eyed awe to suggest their predicament was a special treat. All of the midway's bawdy sights and sounds and smells were still there, but muted, as if he were watching them in a movie.

"Ugh." He edged closer to the seat's center, in the process, pressing even closer to her. "Sorry about this. I'd hoped tonight would be fun, but it's turning out to be a disaster."

"Why, Mr. Buckhorn," she teased, "are you afraid of heights?"

"Nope," he said with a vehement shake of his head.

"So if I made the cart swing, you wouldn't mind?" She bounced just enough to rock them with the magnitude of a 6.0 earthquake.

"Crap on a cupcake," he muttered with a white-knuckled grip on the safety bar, "please stop."

"You are scared." Arm around his shoulders, she gave him a supportive squeeze. "I'm sorry. I shouldn't have pulled that last stunt."

"Might've been nice if you'd skipped it." Teeth gritted, he willed his heart rate to slow. Damned embarrassing was what this was.

"What brought this on?" When Josie took hold of his hands, he focused on her. The sincere warmth behind her brown eyes. The way a light breeze played with her curls. She was country pretty, freckles providing the only makeup needed.

"Wh-when my brothers and I were kids, Wyatt—he's next oldest to me—dared me to jump off the barn roof and into a cattle tank. I'm thinking I must've been around eight or nine, but feeling immortal. I not only took him up on his dare, but broke my right leg in two places. Spent that whole summer cooped up in bed and the damned thing still hurts in the rain." Focusing on Josie's eyes, her soft lips, he forced a breath. "To this day, I can't stand being higher than I sit up on my favorite horse."

"Then why did you suggest riding the tallest ride on the fairgrounds?"

The simple logic behind her question brought on a smile. "Okay," he admitted. "Truth? I wanted to show you how manly I am. But I loused that up good, didn't I?"

"Men…" She laughed, but something about the gesture struck him as sad. "I was more impressed by your recent handling of twin shenanigans than I would ever be by a daredevil stunt—even one as impressive as sitting on an upright track, slowly circling round and round." Her sassy wink told him she was teasing, but her tone implied more.

"Taking a wild stab in the dark," he said, glad for the diversion, "why do I get the feeling you're not all that thrilled with men as a species? Been hurt?"

"More in the realm of pulverized, but let's not ruin our night." Logic would dictate that after such a statement, she'd free her hold on his hands, but instead, she tightened her grip.

"Want me to roughen him up?" Dallas suggested. One thing he never backed down from was a good fight.

"No use. He did the job for you."

Forehead furrowed, he said, "I don't get it."

"Never mind. I shouldn't have said anything."

"But you did." And he needed to know why those few words had her rummaging through her purse for tissue she used to wipe the corners of her eyes.

With a jolt, their car began the long journey down. All of the occupants around them clapped and cheered.

"What a relief, huh?" Josie's smile was forced. Her expression tight, as if the effort of making casual conversation was too much. "Bet you'll be glad to get your feet back on the ground."

A few minutes earlier, he would have, but now, all he wanted was to return light to her eyes.

"How adorable." Josie knelt in front of the 4-H craft display, wondering at all of the work nimble fingers had put into the dollhouse. The home had been outfitted with pint-size solar panels and was part of an exhibit designed to explore nontraditional forms of energy. "I never get tired of seeing what kids can do."

"You seem to have a real affinity for children."

"They're amazing." She studied the bios of the eight fourth-graders who'd worked on the project. "With them you always know where you stand. No mind games."

"Experienced much of that? People messing with your head?"

She shrugged. "Enough to know it sucks."

Moving on to a photo display, he said, "Considering how many times you've dealt with my girls and your recent Ferris wheel rescue of me, I owe you an ear if you ever need anyone to listen."

"Thanks." She angled toward him, fidgeting with her hands. The turn in conversation was awkward to say the least. In fact, the whole night had been forced. Oh—and she wouldn't even try denying that while they'd been crammed together three stories in the air, every time they touched sparked hot, achy awareness she'd rather forget. "Really. But when it comes to personal matters, I prefer keeping them to myself."

"Ouch. I would've liked to think we're friends. Especially since this is our first official date."

"Is that what tonight is?" Two boys ran between them, shooting at each other with wooden rifles. The distraction gave her time to think. "Because the idea of *dating* someone—even a guy as great as you—isn't at all appealing."

Alongside a terrarium loaded with lizards, he froze. "Talk about a ballbuster. That hurts."

"Please don't take it personally. It's not a rejection of you, so much as the principle. I have a hard enough time figuring out what to do with myself, let alone someone else."

"Fair enough. Truthfully, I feel the same. But then chemistry kicks in. Confuses the hell out of me."

Sharply looking away to hide her blush, Josie fought for air. He'd noticed? The way each time they touched the temperature rose by ten degrees? "You're making me uncomfortable."

"Good." They'd wandered into the vegetable area of the show barn. Judging had long since been completed and plates of carrots, zucchinis and green beans were no longer a big draw. Nearly alone in the mammoth space, Dallas stopped in front of her, bracing both of his hands on a display table. He hadn't even touched her, yet his proximity was unbearable. As usual when he was near, caged excitement coursed through her. As if whenever the man was around, *anything* could happen. "It's only fair you be as far from your comfort zone as I am from mine."

"Wh-what's that supposed to mean? Beyond our conversations about Betsy and Bonnie, I hardly even know you."

"Yes, but would you like to? That was kind of the idea behind tonight."

"No," she said, ducking under his arms to escape. "That's not what I want at all. I lead a wonderfully peaceful life—at least I did before your twins took over my classroom."

"Me, too—I mean, my days are all fairly predictable. And that works for me. Only thing not working lately, are my irrational urges to kiss you."

Josie was no medical expert, but didn't people die from racing hearts? Dallas stood miles into her personal space, smelling like every forbidden fruit. Cotton candy. Caramel apples. All things she craved, but as a responsible adult, steered clear of. His warm exhalations teased her upper lip. His blazing blue eyes held an open challenge.

"Please, Josie, tell me I don't want to kiss you."

She gulped. "You don't. For the twins, we should be friends, but nothing more."

"Agreed."

"Th-then why," she asked with hitched breath, "are you still so near?"

"God's honest truth?" He leaned in close enough for her to taste his sweet breath, but then sighed before backing away. "Don't have a clue. But trust me, won't happen again."

"*Oooh,* A BOXED SET OF *Dawson's Creek.*" Josie snatched her treasure before any of her fellow yard sale aficionados had the chance. For only eight on Saturday morning, the crowds were already thick.

"Avoid the topic all you want," Natalie said, having found her own treasure in the form of three wicker baskets. She used them for making care packages for sick coworkers or students whose families could use a little anonymous help. "But mark my words, you're falling for Dallas Buckhorn."

"That's the stupidest thing I've ever heard you say." Josie added a few lightly read picture books to her must-have pile. "I'm not sure how, but Dallas and I have forged a unique friendship."

Natalie snorted. "Based upon mutual hotness?"

Josie hit her over the head with a Thomas the Tank Engine pillow.

"No need for violence," Nat complained, "especially when you know I'm right. You're cute. He's approaching human god status. Whatever you want to label it, you two just might work."

The day was gorgeous. Cool and crisp without a cloud in the sky. So why did her friend seem intent on ruining it? Natalie, better than anyone, knew her past. She knew why Josie had dedicated her life to teaching and helping children while whenever possible avoiding men.

Though Natalie's lighthearted tone told Josie she was kidding, it was hardly a secret that as much as Josie didn't want a romantic entanglement, her friend did. "I've got an even better idea. What if you believe me that I'm not interested in Dallas and you go for him?"

"Nah." Nose wrinkled, Nat said, "Considering how hard he's tried to impress you, what with the ponies and cupcakes and donuts, I think he's all yours."

MONDAY MORNING, JOSIE found herself in the awful position of not only being called to substitute bus duty, but doing it in a relentless downpour. Cold to the point her teeth were chattering, she tried being cheerful about directing shrieking first, second and third graders off their buses and into the school gym. Only two of her students rode the bus and they were both already safely inside.

The few students who walked to school wore rain boots and carried umbrellas. The girls huddled together to stay dry, while the boys pretended they had swords, giving little thought to the fact that they'd be sitting in wet clothes for a good portion of the day.

Traffic for the children whose parents drove them to school was heavy. More than a few wrecks were narrowly avoided and typically well-mannered drivers had resorted to honking and rude gestures in futile attempts to escape the crowded lot.

When a familiar black truck pulled alongside the curb, Josie's stomach lurched.

"Hi, Miss Griffin!" Bonnie, decked out in sunny-yellow rain garb, hopped out. "Betsy lost a tooth."

"I wanted to tell her," Betsy complained, her raincoat, hat and boots pink. "You ruin everything!"

"At least I'm not ugly!" Bonnie hollered.

An ear-splitting whistle came from behind the driver's seat. "Ladies, remember what I told you about bickering? Especially at school. Now, get inside."

"Bye, Daddy," they said in unison, chins drooping.

"Call if they give you any more trouble." Warmth blasted from the truck's heater vents. Even better, was the heat radiating from his smile.

"I will." Why was she suddenly breathless?

"You look cold—but in a cute way."

"Thanks?" Cute was good. At least it had been back in high school. But she felt a million years from that girl.

"Need me to bring you anything? Coffee? Hot cocoa?"

"Sounds delicious, but I'm on duty. Ten more minutes before I can even think about getting warm and dry."

He nodded. "I understand. Well…hope the rest of your day goes better."

"Me, too."

As the crowd dwindled outside, the more Josie was left on her own with her thoughts. Lately, a place she didn't like to be. When she'd seen his truck, she'd dreaded meeting Dallas again. Then he'd wowed her with his smile and she'd been a goner. What was it about the man that left her off balance? Making her doubt her carefully placed emotional walls that thus far had served her so well?

The bell rang, and she no longer had time to think of anything other than squeaky sneakers on the hall floors and her squirming class complaining of being cold and wet. With everyone miserable, she abandoned the usual lesson in favor of story time in the nap corner.

Midway through the tale of a dachshund who hates his brothers and sisters, Natalie entered the room. She carried a steaming, extra-large paper cup from the town's only coffee shop. As surreptitiously as possible with so many eyes on her, she knelt to whisper, "A certain father of twins left this in the office for you. He said seeing you shiver made him sad."

Accepting the drink, sampling it to find hot chocolate so sinfully rich and yummy she felt guilty drinking it in front of her students, Josie tried drawing less attention by getting back to the story. No such luck.

Still in whisper-mode, Nat said, "Care to explain why a guy like Dallas Buckhorn would even care if you're shivering?"

"No."

"What about my dad?" Bonnie asked.

"Nothing, sweetie." Josie cast Nat her most stern Teacher Glare. It only broadened the size of her friend's smile.

"YOU FINALLY WARM?" DALLAS asked when he saw his call was from the girls' school. He assumed it was Josie, because the girls were in music class at this time on a Monday.

"Yes. Anyone ever told you you're crazy sweet?"

"Not lately," he said, followed by a laugh loud enough to startle his horse. With a couple of cows ready to calve, despite the rain, he made the long ride out to the south pasture to check them. He could've driven, but he liked being out on days like this. Made him feel closer to all of the cowboys who'd worked the land before him. "How have my little deviants behaved this morning?"

"Surprisingly well. Ever since leaving the fair, I've expected to be blamed for them having to go home early, but they never said a word about it."

"Good." He pulled down his hat to protect his phone from the rain.

"Where are you? It sounds like you're standing under a waterfall."

"Pretty much sums it up," he said, guiding his horse

beneath a stubby oak. With no lightning, it was as good a place as any to take shelter.

"You're outside?"

"It's my office. Where else would I be?"

"Duh." Her laughter brought out the sun. "Stupid question."

He couldn't resist teasing, "I've always heard there aren't any stupid questions, just stupid people."

After making a cute little growling sound, she sassed, "You're going to pay for that, mister."

"Sounds fun."

"On that note, I need to go make copies. But seriously, thank you for the cocoa."

"It was my pleasure."

Long after hanging up, a sense of well-being stayed with him. At least until his cell rang again an hour later.

"Mr. Buckhorn?" asked a woman whose voice he didn't recognize, though the number was the same as when Josie called.

"Yes."

"This is Marge Honeywell. I'm the school nurse. I have Bonnie in my office and we're afraid she may have a concussion."

Chapter Seven

"It hurts!" Bonnie wailed, breaking Josie's heart.

The tighter the girl clung to her, the more memories of Emma flooded her system. There'd been so much blood. E.R. doctors and nurses had done everything they could, but internal bleeding couldn't be stopped. Josie had known Emma was gone when her arms slipped from around her neck.

The mental image was so striking it stole her breath.

"Miss Griffin, are you okay?" Betsy asked, pressing herself against Josie's left side. "Your face is really white."

"I'm fine," she assured Bonnie's shaken twin.

"Y-you are white," Bonnie managed between hiccupping sobs. "Thank you for saving me." When the girl snuggled still closer, resting her head beneath Josie's chin, the sensation was mesmerizing. It reminded her of how motherhood had changed her in every conceivable way. It'd shown her the magical, healing power of hugs and kisses and tender words. She'd loved Emma to what'd sometimes seemed like an impossible degree. Now that her daughter was gone, Josie knew she never wanted to be a mother again. Suffering another loss would be the end of her.

"You're welcome," Josie said, "but you're going to be fine." The rain had stopped just long enough for the kids to have outside recess. Bonnie had taken the opportunity to once again climb the big tree. This time, however, the bark had been slippery and she'd fallen. In the process, scraping her knees, palms and forearms. She'd also gotten quite a bump to her forehead that was already bruising.

While Josie was busy with the nurse, Natalie was watching her class.

"Bonnie Buckhorn…" Doc Haven, the town's only physician, ambled into Nurse Honeywell's office. "Girl, I believe I've spent the better part of my career patching up your whole family—except for your grandma. She's the only sane one in the bunch."

"You gave us shots," Betsy said. "We don't like you."

The kindly old doctor chuckled. "If I had a nickel for every time I've heard that." Gesturing for the girl to move from Josie's lap to the nurse's exam table, Doc said, "Hop on up here and let me take a look at you."

"No." Bonnie refused to release Josie's neck. "I want Miss Griffin."

"Sweetheart," Josie said, "the doctor needs to check your eyes and head to make sure you aren't seriously hurt. Would it be all right if I carried you to the table?"

"Is he gonna shot me?"

"I don't think so." Looking to the man in question, Josie asked, "Doc Haven? Any shots in this girl's immediate future?"

"I'm sure I could think of something she'd need one for." His wink told Josie and the nurse he was joking, but Bonnie wasn't so sure.

After a thorough exam, the little girl was found to be banged up, but in otherwise good condition. Relief shimmered through Josie, making her ache with wishes that her daughter's diagnosis could've gone so well.

"You okay?" Dallas burst through the door, gaze landing on Bonnie.

"Uh-huh." She raised her arms and he went to her, hugging her against him for all he was worth.

Doc Haven gave Dallas a quick rundown on Bonnie's condition, asked him to keep an eye out for dizziness or nausea, then excused himself to make a house call out to Oak Manor, the town's retirement home.

Josie hadn't thought much about it, but in many ways she and Dallas had similar pasts. Having lost his wife, he knew how tough it was coming back from the dark places a loved one's death can take you. He knew about Hugh—the basics. Like her former husband was dead. But he didn't know how he'd died, and she certainly wasn't ready to share Emma with him—if ever.

"Daddy," Bonnie said, "I was gonna see Mommy in Heaven, but Miss Griffin saved me."

"That was awfully nice of her," he noted with a grateful nod in Josie's direction.

"Yeah," Betsy said, "Bonnie was all upside down and broken, but Miss Griffin came and brought her to the nurse."

"I'm glad." The sight of Bonnie in Dallas's arms and Betsy hugging his legs, knotted Josie's throat. Here was this superrugged cowboy. Every inch manly man from the tip of his hat down to his boots, yet he also had an innate gentleness that appealed to children and apparently kindergarten teachers. Swallowing hard, she looked away. No matter how attractive or kind the man might be, she wasn't falling for him or his mischievous girls. "You know, since Miss Griffin saved Bonnie's life, it might be nice for us to have a party for her. What do you think?"

"Yay!" Betsy danced and Bonnie wriggled. "I love parties!"

"That's not necessary," Josie said. "I would do the same for any student here. All in a day's work."

"Yes," Dallas reasoned, "but on this day, you happened to save *my* student. We'll expect you at the ranch at six Saturday night."

After a full Saturday morning of yard sales in Tulsa, Natalie draped herself across the sofa while Josie grabbed them both Diet Cokes.

"What're you going to wear?" Nat shouted into the kitchen.

"Don't have a clue." Josie handed her friend a drink before collapsing on a lounge chair. "Hasn't the Buckhorn Ranch main house been featured in *Architectural Digest*?"

"Yes, ma'am." Nat sipped her cola. "Best as I can recall, it was back when Duke Buckhorn was still alive. When I was a kid, I remember limos driving in from all over the state, filled with bigwigs heading to their holiday parties. Fourth of July, Christmas, New Year's.

Back then, practically any occasion was a good reason to whoop it up."

"Thanks for the intimidating history lesson, but that doesn't help me with tonight. Are we talking ball gown? Jeans? Church dress?"

"Relax. You're overthinking the whole thing."

"And who made me so stressed? You! My supposed best friend." Natalie looked so innocent, Josie couldn't help but laugh, even though she knew her statement to be true.

"You said you aren't at all attracted to the man or even remotely interested in dating, so what's the big deal? Wear sweats."

"You're a lot of help—*not*. Come on…" Pushing herself upright, she aimed for her bedroom, intent on searching her closet.

Nat followed. "Given any more thought to cleaning out Em's room?"

"Nope." Opening the door to her walk-in closet, Josie pretended her so-called friend hadn't even broached the subject.

"Might be healthy for you."

"Drop it, okay?" Snatching a simple black dress from its hanger, she asked, "How about this? Too fancy? Not fancy enough?"

Lying crossways on the bed, Nat asked, "Have you told Dallas anything about your past?"

"No. Why would I? We're friends. Nothing more."

"Keep telling yourself that and maybe one of these days it'll be true." She rolled over, fluffing her bangs in the mirror.

"Why are you being so mean?" Returning her dress to the rack, Josie joined Nat on the bed.

"I'm sorry." Up on her elbows, she looked to the ceiling. "I worry about you. How you keep your past neatly compartmentalized. But that's not the way life works. It's all interconnected and I wouldn't be a good friend if I encouraged you to keep this up."

"Keep what up? Dallas and I are friends. Nothing more."

"But don't you see that if you'd let go of the past, you two could be more? Josie, you could have a family again. Instead of just pretending to mother your students, you may—"

"Please, go." Bolting upright, Josie folded her arms.

"I'm sorry I hurt you. Really." Nat stood and didn't look the slightest bit apologetic. "But all of that has been on my mind for a while. I want the best for you, and if that means breaking you down in the short run, then so be it."

Once Josie heard Nat close the front door, she threw a pillow at the wall. Damn her. How had the day gone from fun to awful in such a short time? How long had Natalie thought hurtful things about her? Months? Years? Was there a statute of limitations on how long you could mourn your dead child and the man who'd accidentally caused her death before killing himself?

"I HAVEN'T SEEN YOU THIS pumped in forever," Wyatt said, standing alongside him at the poolside grill. Whereas Cash, Dallas and Daisy were blond like their mother had been before turning gray, Wyatt was dark like their dad. Short black hair and brown eyes that kept more secrets than they told.

Sweet scents of barbecued chicken, sausage and ribs rose from the flames while the girls, Cash's wife, Wren, and Josie splashed in the heated pool. With slow country playing on the stereo and fireflies lighting the dark sky, Dallas couldn't remember when he'd last felt so content. Cash was inside, helping their mom bring out potato salad and condiments to the cloth-draped picnic table.

"Gotta say, I'm feeling pretty good." Dallas used tongs to flip the chicken, then brushed on more sauce.

"Josie Griffin have anything to do with that?"

"Maybe." Dallas cast his brother a sly smile. The more he was around Josie, the more he liked her. Trouble was, she reminded him of a skittish colt. He so much as hinted at maybe wanting to be more than friends and she'd bolt.

"She's pretty. Wholesome."

"Yeah, she is."

"Are you gonna go for her?"

"None of your business. Chicken's done. Get me a damned plate."

"Yessir," Wyatt said, tipping his straw cowboy hat's brim.

"Ladies!" Dallas shouted above the splashing in the pool. "We're about ready for dinner."

The twins grumbled, but Wren and Josie helped them dry off, wrapping them sarong-style in thick towels before sitting them at the table. With both women in Buckhorn logo robes, they joined the girls. Wren and

Cash's baby, Robin, was sound asleep in her blanket-covered carrier.

"Here we go." Georgina set a bowl of pasta salad and napkin-wrapped silverware on the table. "Who's hungry?"

"Me!" Betsy cried.

"Me, too!" Bonnie was never one to be outdone.

"Thank you for putting on such a beautiful spread." Josie forked a chicken breast onto her plate. "This all looks delicious."

"Dallas does amazing things with his grill," his mom said. "His kielbasa is always perfectly done. A little hard on the outside, but soft and juicy inside. Overall, a really lovely taste."

"That's enough about my sausage." A glance toward Josie showed her eyes to be smiling.

"I don't know…" Cash speared his meat, holding up the link for all to view. "My wife has always enjoyed a nice, long sausage over the more stubby varieties."

Wren elbowed his ribs. "You're horrible."

"Yeah, but I'm damned good-looking and all yours, my beauty." When Cash kissed his wife, Dallas fought a jealous twinge. All of a sudden, he missed what his brother had—not his striking good looks, self-confidence or playful attitude that drew folks in like moths to a flame, but the intimacy he and Wren shared. The turning over in the middle of the night and having someone he loved right there beside him. He wanted it with a keen, cutting edge that tore through him, but he'd already had his chance at love and had lost.

"Earmuffs," Josie said to the twins, laughing along with Wren.

"Huh?" Having been so engrossed in buttering her corn cob, Bonnie had missed the entire conversation.

Betsy raised her chin. "Uncle Cash was being bad and Aunt Wren had to yell at him."

"Oh." Used to this occurrence, Bonnie returned her attention to flavoring her corn.

With dinner finished, the girls grew bored with conversations centered on brood mares and how late in the season they were in baling the hay in the east pasture. With them scurrying off to their playhouse, Dallas's mom opened white wine for the ladies and Wyatt grabbed beers for the guys.

"Thought Henry was joining us?" Wyatt helped himself to the few potato chips left in the bowl.

Cash shrugged. "I told him. Don't know what he could've found more exciting than hanging with us."

"More exciting than you, hon?" Wren pushed up from the table's bench. Robin had started to fuss. "Dominoes? Reading the phone book?"

"Ha, ha." Cash stood to help her while together they cooed over their creation. "Somebody's sleepy."

"Me," Wren admitted with a yawn. She wore her long, red hair in a high ponytail. Throw in her freckles and she looked all of twelve. As an intern at Saint Francis Hospital in Tulsa, she worked long enough hours that she was sometimes forced to stay over. This was one of her rare free weekends.

"I guess since my glass is empty, I'll head off to bed,

too." His mom hugged Josie. "It was so nice meeting you. Please come again soon."

"Thank you." Josie smiled.

With Cash and Wren making their goodbyes, that left Dallas alone with Josie and Wyatt.

Dallas's younger brother cleared his throat. "Now that I'm officially the third wheel, how about I track down your girls and put them to bed."

"Sounds great to me. Thanks, man."

"No problem."

"Should we clean up this mess?" Josie asked, surveying what little was left from dinner.

"Probably, but I'd rather take our drinks over to that lounger." He nodded toward the cushioned seat built for two. On his way to the girls' playhouse, Wyatt had lit the built-in gas torches. Combined with the glowing pool lights, though the evening had turned nippy, the patio flowers were still fragrant and lush. His brother had also put on one of Cash's Garth Brooks compilation CDs. Countless times, Cash bragged he'd never used it without sealing the deal.

"It's getting late. I probably should just head home."

After consulting his watch, Dallas said, "It's nine-thirty and not even a school night."

"True, but…" Standing, she reached for the empty potato salad dish.

He stood, too, promptly taking it from her, putting the bowl back on the table. "Play with me. It'll be fun."

"The word isn't in my vocabulary."

Shifting deeper into her personal space, he asked, "Play? Fun? Be?"

"Stop." Her breathless giggle told him he was on the right track.

"Why?" Taking her hands, he placed them around his neck. His hands low on her hips, he swayed her in time to the music.

"Dallas…"

"You look awfully cute in that robe." He especially liked her messy pile of crazy-corkscrew hair. How the deep V at her throat guided his eyes to naughty places.

"I'm thirty-three. Hardly in the right age bracket for cute."

"Says who?" Pulling her close enough that even air couldn't squeeze between them, he nuzzled her neck.

"Dallas, please…" She made a halfhearted effort to push him away, but then he slipped his hand beneath her chin, drawing her lips to his. Their kiss was awkward and tender and the most exciting thing to happen to him in years. "…I can't."

"Why?" Dallas kissed her again, this time around, increasing the pressure, the heat. "Afraid the principal's hiding in the bushes and she'll jump out to give you detention?"

She laughed, but tears formed in her eyes and spilled down her cheeks.

"Hey…" Brushing them with the pads of his thumbs, he asked, "What's this about? There's no crying when I'm trying to get some action."

"I—I know," she said with a sniffle. "Sorry. This is embarrassing."

"No, no I get it. Sort of." He knew the right thing

to do was to release her, but instead, he hugged her for all he was worth. He stroked her hair. Whispered that everything would be all right even though he didn't even know what was wrong.

"You're the first person I've kissed since…" Fisting his T-shirt, she admitted, "And I liked it. I mean really liked it. But that's awful. You're a parent to two of my students and—"

"Whoa." Cupping his hands to her tear-stained cheeks, he pressed his lips to hers. When she moaned, he took the opportunity to stroke her tongue with his. "You're too beautiful to cry."

"I'm not," she insisted while he danced her to the chaise.

"You so are…" Guiding her down, he stretched out alongside her, kissing her again, slipping his hand inside her robe, sweeping her collarbone and shoulder. Lowering the robe, he brushed his lips along the trail his fingers had just blazed. Her skin called to mind the softest satin. Cool and smooth and inviting.

"I—I should go," she murmured.

"Later. Now, you have to keep kissing me."

She nodded and then shook her head. "There's so much about me you don't know."

"But I want to. Tell me everything."

"Maybe…" She kissed him again. "I wish I could abandon all that I am. I want to let go of the past—keep the good, but the rest…" She sharply exhaled, leading him to believe her convictions weren't as strong as she claimed. "Do you ever wish you could just delete the past from your brain as easily as a corrupt file from your computer?"

"Sure," he admitted. "Doesn't everyone? But, Josie, your past made you who you are. And I like this woman."

"I—I like you, too. I only wish things could be different—I could be different." Gathering her robe at her throat, she scooted off the lounger, scurrying toward the changing room.

"Josie, wait!" Chasing after her, he stood outside.

When she emerged, fully clothed in her jeans and a sweater and the red boots that'd been one of the first things that had attracted him to her, he searched for the right thing to say, only it wouldn't come. Why?

No doubt because she was right. He'd been a fool to kiss her. She was his daughters' teacher. A friend. Nothing more.

Extending her hand for him to shake, she said, "I had fun. Thank you."

"You're welcome."

Gesturing toward the dinner remains still littering the table, she asked, "Want me to help clean before I go?"

"I'm good. Might even leave it till in the morning."

"Aren't you worried about bugs or possums?"

"Not so much." How in the hell had they gone from kissing to a topic so mundane as night creatures licking the crumbs off their plates? He wanted more from her, but what? Clearly, they shouldn't be physical. But as friends, he'd welcome emotional depth.

"What are you thinking?" she asked. He fought the urge to trace the furrow between her eyes.

He shook his head. "Nothing important. Come on, let me walk you to your car." *And tomorrow, with any luck, I'll wake having forgotten your taste.*

Chapter Eight

"I want details." While her students were in music late Monday morning, Shelby popped into Josie's classroom. "How was the ranch? Everything it's made out to be?"

"Better. Only the curious thing is that I'd expected his family to be snobby—you know, like the stereotypical rich TV ranch family. But in reality, they were all genuinely nice people." Especially Dallas. How long would it take for her to stop reliving their steamy kisses every time she closed her eyes?

"Mmm, sounds dreamy. And here I sat at home with a Lifetime movie and a Lean Cuisine."

Josie couldn't help but smile. "What a coincidence. That perfectly describes most of my weekends."

"Seeing him again?"

"No." Worrying her lower lip, Josie contemplated asking her friend if it was wrong that she wanted to see him again. But why ask when Josie already knew the answer? "Neither of us is looking for anything beyond friendship."

Shelby wrinkled her nose. "He's great-looking, seems

nice, has two adorable kids and is probably one of the richest guys in the state. What's the problem with a little canoodling?"

Sighing, Josie admired the diligence of her hard-working kiddos. They were drawing the state of Oklahoma and then adding elements such as the state flower and bird. "When I'm at school, I feel energized. Excited about what I do. But in my personal life…" She frowned. "Nat and I got in a huge fight Saturday afternoon. She thinks I should clear out Emma's room."

"What do you think?"

"I can't even imagine such a thing. Hugh made it somewhat easy on me. I was so angry over him taking his own life that I wanted to get rid of most of his stuff just to put that rage behind me. With Em, it's different. I can't let go."

"Who says you have to?" Sipping at fragrant coffee from the mug she cradled, she added, "Do you honestly think that remodeling her room is going to erase her from your memory?"

"Of course not."

"There's your answer."

"Miss Gwiffin." Thomas waved his paper in the air. "I forgot the bird."

"That's why I put a hint on the Smart Board." She pointed to the front of the room where an oversize image of a scissor-tailed flycatcher standing on the side of a country road was meant for the kids to use as a visual aid.

"Oh!" His big grin lit her heart.

"He's crazy-cute. If only being a grown-up was as simple, huh?" Shelby finished off her coffee.

"True."

THOUGH JOSIE WAS STILL HURT by Natalie's speech, she also found herself in need of educated advice. Which was why, instead of spending lunch in her room sorting papers, she stood outside of Nat's office, waving a Diet Coke still cold from the vending machine. "Truce?"

"No bribes necessary," Natalie declared from behind her desk, wagging her own can, "but I will take a hug."

"Sorry I snapped at you," Josie confessed.

"Sorry I lectured you." Natalie put extra oomph into her hug. "You didn't need that on top of everything else you're going through."

"But that's just it," she said, occupying the nearest of Nat's two guest chairs. "I love my life. Granted, there isn't a day that passes when I don't still miss my daughter, but overall, I have a lot to be thankful for. A great job and supportive friends. Plenty of food in my belly and a roof over my head. Before meeting Dallas, I felt satisfied, but now…"

Nat gasped. "You sly fox. You kissed him, didn't you?"

"Technically," Josie said with a misty smile, "he kissed me, but then the lines of who did what to whom got blurred."

"Do tell." Leaning forward with her elbows on a pile of manila folders, she asked, "How far are we talking? First, second, third base?"

"Second. Get your mind out of the gutter. But what would you think if I confessed to wanting more? Am I a horrible person?"

Snorting, Nat said, "That's the stupidest question I've ever heard. Why—for even a second—would you think you're not entitled to each second of happiness you can catch?"

"Guilt, I suppose." Worrying the cuticle on her thumb, she admitted, "There's a part of me that feels traitorous for indulging in purely selfish pleasures. I mean, enjoying my work with students is one thing, but sampling Dallas Buckhorn's physical attributes felt like an all-out sin."

"Good." Straightening, Nat clapped her hands. "Love the sound of that. Now, all you have to do is call him."

Josie shook her head. "I told you—and him—I'm not interested. Outside of school, I'm not seeing him again."

"DADDY?" SATURDAY MORNING, Dallas woke to Betsy peering at him from the foot of his bed.

"Hey, peanut." His eyes barely working, he asked, "What's wrong? Why are you up so early?"

"I think I'm going to—" She threw up. Everywhere. On his comforter. The carpet. Herself.

"Oh, baby." Going to her, he scooped her into his arms, carrying her to the big soaking tub in his room that she loved. Once he turned on the faucets, adjusting the water just right and then dumping in half a bottle of grape-scented bubbles, he tugged off her smelly, wet clothes before lifting her into the tub. "Poor thing. Did you eat anything weird last night?"

She shook her head.

"Daddy?" Behind him, Bonnie strolled up, her cheeks feverish and pink. "My stomach really—" Quick reflexes got his eldest daughter to the toilet before he had another mess to clean.

With both girls lounging up to their necks in bubbles, he jogged down the hall for cleaning supplies.

"DAAADDY!"

Dallas jogged back to his bathroom to find Betsy wrapped in a towel and hunched over the toilet.

"Good grief, baby…" He rubbed her back. "Think I should sell you and get a new kid who's healthy?"

"You're mean."

"Oh, I was teasing, Miss Sensitivity. You know how much I love you."

She retched again.

Mind reeling, Dallas wasn't sure of his next step. This was the kind of thing Stella or his mom would handle. But with both women gone—his mother on a weekend garden tour in Eureka Springs, Arkansas—he was on his own. Not good, considering that beyond the basics, he didn't know diddly about the girls' medical issues.

That fact served as yet one more reminder of what a crappy father he was. Despite the fact, he knew he was in over his head, and when it came to the twins' well-being, he wasn't opposed to asking for help.

Stepping into the hall, he punched Josie's number into his cell. She answered on the third ring.

"Hey," he said, not wasting time on pleasantries.

"I've got an emergency here at the ranch. Mind helping out?"

After hearing a recap of the morning's events, Josie said, "Hang tight. I'll be right there."

INDIAN SUMMER HAD BEEN overtaken by a cool drizzle that suited Josie's mood. It wasn't that she minded helping Dallas and his girls, but she did wonder why, when he was surrounded by family, he'd called her.

After dressing in a comfy jogging suit, the trip to the ranch took under twenty minutes.

Dallas opened the door for her, ushering her inside. "Thank goodness you're here."

"If the twins are this sick, why haven't you called a doctor?"

"I'm guessing they have a flu bug, but I don't know the first thing to do. Last night, Mom took off for the weekend and the girls have been tag-teaming me for an hour."

"If it is a virus, hopefully they'll soon have it out of their systems. Have you taken their temperatures?"

"Can't find a thermometer."

"You really are clueless." Slipping off her lightweight jacket, she hung it on a brass hook on the wall. Dallas's dirty-blond hair stuck out at crazy angles and his jaw sported a dark shadow. Dressed in navy flannel PJ bottoms and a white T-shirt that hugged his muscular chest, her mouth went dry from the mere sight of him. What would it be like to have touching privileges? To be able to run her hands along his hard ridges any time she caught the fancy? Forcing her mind back to the matter at hand, she asked, "Where are the patients?"

"Right this way." He shyly extended his hand, and she took it, feeling all of thirteen due to shivery excitement stemming from just his touch. What was happening to her? She was a sensible, grown woman never prone to flights of fancy. *Practical* might as well be her middle and last name. A fling with Dallas would only bring her pain.

True, her conscience conceded, but in the short run, it could also produce an insane amount of pleasure.

"Miss Griffin!" Betsy and Bonnie jumped to the foot of Dallas's bed for hugs.

Bonnie quickly turned green and kept on jumping right off the bed for a run into the bathroom.

Josie chased after her, holding her shoulders. "Sweetie, you're a mess."

"What about me?" Betsy asked. "Am I a mess, too?"

"Absolutely." Josie took a washcloth from a pile of them tucked into a linen nook. Wetting it with cold water, she held it to Bonnie's forehead. "There you go," she soothed. "I know it hurts, but the more you get out, the faster you'll feel better. All of the bugs have to go away."

"I have bugs?"

"Sort of." Easing onto the cool tile floor alongside the commode, Josie drew the girl onto her lap, gently rocking. How many times had she held Emma like this? Truth be told, being a mom again—even on a temporary basis—felt amazing. "Teeny tiny germs get into your body and cause all sorts of trouble. That's why it's important to wash your hands a lot—especially this time of year."

"Oh." Bonnie leaned back against her, obviously exhausted.

"I like washing my hands and playing with the soap," Betsy exclaimed. "I like to squirt out lots of soap so it looks like slimy boogers between my fingers."

"That's gross," Bonnie said.

"I agree." Josie hugged her tighter, relishing the sensation, however long it lasted. Her emotions battled, but for now at least, the pleasurable present won over her painful past. It broke her heart to see Bonnie so ill, but to be needed again on such a basic level was bliss. "But at least it gets your sister nice and squeaky clean."

Betsy made a face. "I *don't* squeak!"

It took a while but the twins finally stopped throwing up. Josie tucked them into bed, and with both girls sleeping, she dared leave their side.

Dallas entered his room, thermometer in hand. "Found it in Mom's room."

When he offered it to her, she waved it away. "I've felt enough feverish bodies to guess they're running a tad over a hundred. Besides, with the girls finally resting, I'd hate to wake them."

Nodding, he said, "Sounds reasonable." After a moment's awkward silence, he said, "Thanks for coming. I know I could've handled this on my own, but it seemed too overwhelming."

Gesturing for him to follow her into the hall, she whispered, "I understand the first few months of school can be daunting but, Dallas, helping your children when they're sick is a pretty basic parenting skill." One she'd learned early on with her own daughter.

Scowling, he said, "I'm a horrible father. I get it. You don't have to rub it in."

"I'm not." But was she? She'd move heaven and earth if given one more second with Emma. Here, Dallas had been given the gift of two precious children, yet he didn't seem to realize how lucky he was.

Heels of his hands on his forehead, eyes closed, he suggested, "Feel free to take off. I'll handle things from here."

"Don't be like that."

"What did you expect?" Arms now tightly folded, he refused to meet her stare.

"Not for you to pout like one of your girls over a little constructive criticism."

Still beyond miffed by Josie's lack of support, Dallas led her toward his mother's favorite room.

His mom loved to read, so his father had the library built just for her. Ten-foot shelves lined one wall, a half wall overlooked the living room and the third wall consisted of custom paned windows that towered toward the ceiling's peak. Lounge chairs and ottomans provided comfortable seating while side tables held his father's statuary bronze lamp collection which illuminated pages with just the right amount of light. A study table built from a massive redwood slab had served him and his brothers and sister through too many term papers to count.

"This is amazing," Josie noted, staring up in awe. Six skylights provided an abundance of natural light.

"The more I see of this house, the more I understand why everyone in town talks about it."

"I've never really thought about it, but yeah. Guess I'm lucky to have grown up here." The chair he sat in had a Sharpie stain on the rolled arm. Wyatt had been grounded for a week once their mother found out he'd tattooed the dog with the same pen. "How about you?" he forced himself to ask if for no other reason than to prove that as a grown man, he certainly didn't pout. "Where are your roots?"

"Here and there. I was born in Michigan, but spent most of my life in Oklahoma City. My husband's first job out of college was for the First National Bank of Weed Gulch. When I landed a position with the school, we felt as if our every dream had come true."

"How did he die?" The second Dallas asked the question, he regretted it. Her complexion paled as she pressed her lips into a thin line. "Not that it's any of my business."

"He shot himself."

"Holy shit," he blurted without thinking. "You're that guy's wife? I remember when it happened." The man used his grandfather's shotgun to do the deed. If memory served him right, Josie had been the one to find him. For a town the size of Weed Gulch, such shocking news traveled like wildfire, though Dallas by no means knew everyone.

Sharply looking away, she said, "You were right. I should go." She stood, but with his hands to her shoulders, he urged her down.

"Sorry. My question was innocent enough. Last thing I intended was to dredge up an awful time."

"I appreciate your apology, but it's best I go." This time when she stood, he didn't stop her.

Hands in his pockets, he admitted, "I—I don't know what to say."

"No one does." Already on the stairs, she beat him to the bottom.

Chasing, he tried stopping her from taking her jacket from the wall peg, but was too late. "Please, stay. I'm a pig."

"Far from it. To the contrary, I'm a woman whose husband was so desperate to escape her he put a bullet in his head."

Chapter Nine

Josie escaped to her car with Dallas running barefoot after her. "Get back in the house," she barked. "Your girls are alone."

"Just this once, they'll survive." He braced his hands on her car door. "Right now, you're my main concern. You can't drop a bombshell like that and then run."

"Watch me." She started the engine.

"Knock it off. Why the hell are you pissed? I asked a legit question, you told me the answer. End of story. We never need speak of it again."

"Just because we're not talking about it," she snapped, gripping the steering wheel with all of her might, "doesn't mean what Hugh did isn't always going to be with me. His blood has become a stain on my soul." She wasn't upset with Dallas, she was grateful to him for jolting her back to reality. She'd enjoyed feeling needed. Too much. Lounging in a big, comfy bed with an attractive man and his girls had been like fate waving a huge, red warning flag smack in front of her face.

Don't get too close.

"Josie, please… Sure, I'd like to talk this out, but beyond that, I still need help with the girls."

Exasperated with this man who was incapable of doing a task as simple as holding comforting cool cloths to his daughters' heads, Josie shot him a look of raw disgust before aiming her car away from his maddeningly handsome face.

"HENRY," DALLAS SAID as he entered the barn office later that afternoon. The twins had slept off whatever had been ailing them and, after having them checked out by Wren, he'd helped saddle their ponies. Though low clouds hugged brown earth, the air smelling of wet leaves and straw, Dallas figured fresh air never did a body harm. "That woman's maddening as they come."

"Which one?" Henry asked, not looking up from whittling the body of a toy car. By each Christmas, he'd made dozens of them for a local church. The guy loved kids, and it warmed Dallas's heart that the same man who'd been a friend and confidant to him while growing up was now doing the same for the next generation of Buckhorns. "Ask me, any female over the age of ten is more trouble than she's worth."

Glancing up from the feed order, Dallas chuckled. "That's just because you've yet to find a woman who'd have you."

The old coot shook his hat-covered head.

"Anyway, I was talking about the girls' teacher."

"Pretty thing." He chipped off the portion of the pine block he'd use as a fender. "Like that mess of red hair."

"Me, too." Alas, she also possessed a forked tongue with the venom to match.

"So what's your problem?" He set his work aside on a battered leather trunk filling in as a side table. Using a whisk broom, he made quick work of cleaning his mess. "It's fixin' to rain again and I figure I'd better wrangle down the twins."

"I'll get them," Dallas volunteered, still fuming from Josie's digs at his daddy skills. "And, anyway, all I was gonna say is that the woman makes me crazy. One minute, running hot. Next, biting like a January wind."

Shrugging, Henry tipped his hat. "Ask me, you're better off on your own." Alongside the desk, the grizzled cowboy patted Dallas's back. "Come on. We'll get the girls in together, then have that sister-in-law of yours watch them while we grab a couple beers."

"BET YOU TEN BUCKS YOU won't climb that sexy behind up on the pool table and give us a dance."

"Oh." Josie tipped back the remains of her rum and Coke, flashing the cowboy at the bar her brightest smile. "After I've had a few more of these, I'll take you up on that bet and raise you twenty." Remington's Bar and Motel out by the toll road had a reputation around Weed Gulch for being the kind of establishment ladies didn't frequent, but so far, Josie had found all of the men to be extraordinarily nice—unlike Dallas.

With honky-tonk country music blaring from the jukebox, she ordered another drink before hopping down from her barstool to dance. Her favorite red boots stood out in stark contrast against the wood floor, making her giggle. Dancing was fun!

Someone in the growing crowd wolf whistled, only spurring her on. Removing the ponytail holder that held her hair, she bent at her waist, flipping her curls down and back, giving them a good shake. If these boys wanted a show, she wouldn't disappoint. Hugh might not have wanted her, but there were plenty of other men who'd be proud to have her for their girl.

Music pumping, she unbuttoned the top of her plaid blouse, showing just enough cleavage to tease before undoing the bottom as well, tying the tails halter style.

"Take it all off!" A man in the crowd shouted.

"You wish," she teased with a flirty sashay of her prairie skirt. "But if one of you bring me another rum and Coke with extra cherries, you might just get an extra-warm thank-you in return."

"Woo-hoo!" several men shouted, pumping their fists.

"Someone get this girl more rum!" a T-shirt-wearing trucker shouted. "We've got us a stripper ready to go!"

Swaying her hips in smooth figure eights while her audience cheered, Josie had just bent low enough to give the men in the front row more to cheer about when the music abruptly stopped.

"What gives?" one guy who'd been especially into her show groused.

Parting the crowd was Dallas.

Standing a good six inches taller than any of the men

around him, the stony set of his jaw told all assembled to steer clear.

"Josie." He grated his words from between clenched teeth. "You need to get the hell out of here."

"Make me," she taunted with a shake of her hips.

Growling, he stepped up, grasped her about the thighs and swung her over his shoulder with no more care than if she'd been a feed sack bound for the horse barn.

"Put me down!" she shrieked, pummeling and kicking as he swept her through the gaping crowd.

"Hey!" the trucker protested. "Bring her back! This was just getting good!"

Ignoring the many complaints, as well as her continued shrieking, Dallas marched right out the door. Once he'd crossed from the bar lot over to the motel's, he finally set Josie to her feet. "What the hell kind of stunt were you pulling? You're a freakin' kindergarten teacher. Aren't you right up there on the virgin meter next to nuns?"

"News flash," Josie said, hands on her hips, "but I'm a grown woman and if I want to dance in a honky-tonk or anywhere else, I damn well will."

He winced. "No cussing from you, either—and button your shirt."

Raising her chin, she sassed, "I will cuss and strip whenever and wherever I like, thank you very much."

"Look, I did you a favor. Do you really want some clown chronicling your striptease on his phone, then posting it on the Web for the world to see?"

"Like that would ever happen. I was just having fun."

"Taking off your clothes?" Growling in frustration, he tossed his head back. "You're a disaster. How much have you had to drink?"

Giggling, she admitted, "Two. The cherries were *really* yummy."

"Uh-huh…" Glancing about the empty parking lot, he said, "Let's get you home."

"No." After stomping her foot to show him she meant business, she turned back to the bar. "I came here to find a man who won't hurt me, and I'm not leaving till I do."

Dragging her back by her shirtsleeve, he asked, "Of all places in Oklahoma to find a man, why here?"

Biting her lower lip to keep it from trembling, she shifted her weight from one foot to the other. "I already went the traditional route—marrying a guy from college. You know what happened there. I've dated around, but they were all duds. Then there's you—has there *ever* been a bigger walking disaster?"

"Me?" He coughed. "I must need a few more shots of whiskey, because I thought you just said I'm not date worthy."

"Oh—I did." Her exaggerated nod made her yawn. Who knew dancing could be such hard work? "You're a lousy parent, don't appreciate even half of the blessings you've been given—worst of all…" she made a drum beat on the battered Ford pickup alongside her "…you're a tease."

"E-excuse me?"

"Oh—don't go pretending you don't know what I'm talking about. The night I shared dinner with your family, and then we played Five Minutes in Heaven by the pool, you kissed me breathless. You kissed me until I was consumed with nothing but horrible thoughts of having you inside me, but—" Lowering her voice, she asked, "Wanna know a secret?"

Arms crossed, Dallas leaned on a Chevy and said, "Why not?"

"I'm a kindergarten teacher. I'm not supposed to even know naughty things, let alone think them! It's bad. Very, very bad. And, anyway, since you're a horrible tease, I suspect you don't even know how to *truly* please a woman."

"That a challenge?" The bar door opened and three drunken rednecks spilled out, carrying with them laughter and the chorus of a country song about whiskey making you frisky. "'Cause if it is…" He crossed to her Ford, bracing his hands on the front fender, effectively, deliciously, caging her in. "I'm more than happy to grab us a room and show you just how wrong you are."

"Big words, cowboy, but I'm not seeing a lot of follow-through." What she was getting was an awful lot of quivery, hot sensations overriding the alcohol. Somewhere far in the back of her head, a voice reasoned to call Natalie for a ride home to sleep it off. But how could she possibly do that when a cowboy of epic proportions stood close enough for her to realize the bulge pressing against her midsection was in no way the proverbial flashlight.

Tugging her toward him, he asked, "You sure this isn't just booze talking?"

"Only thing I'm sure of is that even though you annoy

and infuriate me, for some unfathomable reason you still turn me on—despite not being able to deliver."

"Oh—if that's what you want, sugar, that's exactly what you're gonna get." He kissed her hard, but then soft, dizzying her with the sweep of his tongue. Suddenly too warm clothes left little to the imagination. It was no secret he wanted her and Josie was hot for him, too. Abruptly sober, tired of being the perpetual good girl, Josie abandoned everything she knew to be right and so-called decent in favor of unbuckling Dallas's big, silver belt buckle. Still kissing, she unfastened the button on his jeans, lowering the zipper to set him free.

He felt like hot, silken steel and she wanted him inside her with a ferocity that bordered on madness. Her rum buzz had been replaced by plain old lust. Breasts swelling and aching against his chest, she wanted to forget all worries and focus on the here and now. On the sensations flooding her limbs with devil-may-care pleasure.

Hefting her skirt, tearing her thong only to let it fall to the gravel lot, Dallas rasped, "Let's get this party started."

Cloaked in the shadows, he lifted her, urging her legs around him. Hands gripping her buns, he slid her onto his erection. She gasped from his initial size, but then opened, taking him in, making them one.

Her backside cold against the Ford, the front of her felt superheated, clinging to him, trusting him to make everything better.

Lowering his mouth to her chest and then breasts, he sucked, biting through her lacy bra. Nipples hard, raw with sensation, his actions only worsened the wondrous tension building within her.

In and out he thrust with her clinging, clawing his back with her hands beneath his shirt. When the pleasure-pain was nearly too much to bear, white-hot heat drowned her in its light.

He tensed and then shuddered, with the bulk of her weight still resting on the truck, he nuzzled her neck, moving his attentions upward, ultimately landing on swollen lips.

"Take it back," he said, voice still sex-raspy.

"What?" she teased, knowing full well what he meant. The man might be a lot of things, but in this particular area, he'd more than delivered.

His growl culminated in another kiss that rocketed to her toes. "We're going to regret this in the morning."

With him still inside her, she refused to think further than the next few seconds in his arms.

"I already do," she admitted, yanking her skirt back to a decent level once he'd landed her on her feet. "I don't know what came over me."

"Judging by your taste, rum," Dallas mumbled, zipping his fly. "In my case, beer."

While each fumbled with the business of straightening their clothes, Josie fought the niggling fear that not only had she made a fool of herself, but she was also on the verge of being sick. What had she done? Why? Was she really so hard up for validation?

"I'm sorry," Dallas finally said, kicking gravel with the toe of his boot. "I never meant for this to happen—"

"I feel the same. Trust me, we need never speak of it again."

An audible sigh told the story of his relief. "You're in no shape to drive. Can I give you a lift? My ranch foreman will handle getting your car home."

Wanting to refuse, Josie mumbled her thanks, knowing Dallas was just being practical.

What she couldn't say—would *never* say—was that no matter how ill-advised their actions had just been, she feared it would be a good long while before she forgot his feel and taste. A horrible fate, considering she never wanted to see or think of the man again!

Chapter Ten

"You okay?" Monday morning, Nat stood behind Josie in the school cafeteria lunch line. "The look of death doesn't become you."

Josie shot her supposed friend a dirty look.

Nat took an apple from the fruit bar. "Don't suppose your gray complexion and bloodshot eyes have anything to do with dancing at Remington's?"

Beyond mortified, not to mention still hungover, Josie focused on the chicken stir-fry Paula had put on her plastic tray.

"Mike—that UPS guy I've been seeing—was there. Said you put on quite a show."

"Remind me at the end of this school year to move. I'm tired of my private life being everyone's business."

Nat thanked Paula for her loaded tray. "Then you probably don't want to hear that gossip also has it that you and Dallas disappeared for a good thirty minutes out in the parking lot. Or that his ranch foreman drove your car home."

"Shh…" Turning her attention to Paula, Josie said, "I'll have green beans, too, please."

"The rumors are true?" The cafeteria worker's grin was even cheesier than Nat's. "You and Dallas Buckhorn are, like, a couple?"

"Of course not." How upset would Josie's principal be if she up and quit midyear? Not only didn't she frequent Remington's, but she definitely had never indulged in a parking lot liaison. Worse yet, Josie's mind refused to stop replaying the mortifying public tryst. Memories brought with them the scorching brand of Dallas's fingertips on her behind.

"She'll deny it," Nat said, adding her apple to her filled tray, "but check out those red cheeks. I'm telling you—something's up."

Josie elbowed her friend's ribs. "Knock it off. I'm as single as they come and planning to stay that way."

"Boo."

In line at Weed Gulch's only combination gas and convenience store, Josie spun around to face Dallas in all of his glory. "It's you."

"Oh, come on," he leaned low to whisper in her ear, in the process sending a myriad of shivers through her, "play nice. We shared a moment. That's all. We still have the rest of the girls' school year to get through."

"With that in mind," she fairly hissed, praying no one either of them knew witnessed their scene as they moved up in line, "I think it best we only see each other in a school setting." A week had passed since she'd last seen him, yet as far as her body was concerned it might as well have been mere seconds. He hadn't so much as grazed her, yet her whole body hummed.

Outside, she'd filled her car's tank, paying at the pump. Her only item was a twelve-pack of Sprite.

"Let me carry that for you." Without asking, Dallas took it from her, setting his own supersize pack of beef jerky on top.

Irritable and feeling achy all of a sudden, Josie grumbled, "I managed just fine on my own, thank you very much."

"Of course, you did." He winked and her stomach fluttered in response. "But would it kill you to let a guy be a gentleman?"

"No." But at the rate her pulse raced from his mere proximity—yes, technically, she may die. But oh, what a way to go. She'd forgotten his sheer size. The breadth of his shoulders and slightly bowlegged walk, as if he'd spent so much time on a horse, that even while standing on solid ground he craved being in his saddle. Reminding herself further nonprofessional fraternization between them would be ill-advised, Josie was beyond thrilled to have made it to the front of the line. "Could I please have my pop?"

He set it on the counter, but insisted on paying.

Though she thanked him, back at the pumps, she asked, "Was that necessary? What if someone had seen? What don't you get about the fact that I don't want to be associated with you."

He set the case atop her car. "Hell, woman, it's just soda. Nothing to get your panties in a wad about, because trust me, last thing I need—or want—is one more female messing with my life."

"No." Bonnie stomped her feet and clamped her mouth shut.

"Daddy," Betsy announced from in front of the twins' double bathroom vanity, "that means she's not going to brush her teeth tonight because the toothpaste is poison."

"That's stupid." Dallas flipped open the lid to the bubble gum sparkle flavor he'd bought specifically because Bonnie had wanted it. Taking a whiff, he noted, "Smells good to me—like a wad of that stuff you chew every day."

"It tastes icky and I won't stick it in my mouth." And to prove it, she ripped it from Dallas's hand only to toss it in the toilet.

"Oooh," Becky said. "You're in trouble."

Dallas's first instinct was to call for his mother. Then he was wishing for Stella to return.

Bonnie propped her little fists on her hips and raised her chin, challenging him with a ghostly blue-eyed stare he hadn't seen for five agonizing years. If for only an instant, Bobbie Jo returned in the little girl their love had created. And it physically, emotionally, drove him to his knees.

"Daddy?" Betsy wrapped her arms around him in a hug. "Are you crying?"

Swiping tears he'd never wanted his girls to see, he said, "Nope. I'm just fine, and Bonnie's going to stick her hand in the toilet and get the toothpaste. She's then going to muck stalls until she's earned enough money to pay for it."

"Am not! Am not! Am not!" After screaming her declaration at him, she ran for her room.

"Oooh." Betsy shook her head. "Now she's *really* gonna get it."

"Go to bed," Dallas said wearily.

Betsy scampered off, and he completed Bonnie's task, washed his hands then pondered heading to her room to lecture her, but on what? He had never missed his wife more. When it came to raising their girls, he suddenly felt as if he was failing miserably. When had they changed from adorable munchkins to monsters?

Before their wild night, Dallas would've asked Josie for help, but now that he recognized just how little self-control he had in keeping his hands off her, he felt powerless in that arena, as well.

Maybe someday he'd be ready for a second shot at love, but for now, becoming the father Bobbie Jo had trusted him to be was his number-one goal.

OF ALL THE ROTTEN LUCK...

Dallas stood in the candy aisle of Mefford's—the town's only pharmacy. Surveying the antacids in the next section was Josie. Outside, the wind was fiendish and her red corkscrew curls formed a sexy-as-hell mane. The cold had pinkened her cheeks and the lips that still haunted his every daydream.

Hoping to avoid the woman, Dallas took the long way to the checkout, down the bandage and corn pad aisle. Too bad for him, Josie must've used the same tactic. Her furrowed brows told him she was just as annoyed by another chance meeting as him.

"Fancy meeting you here," he said with what he hoped came off as a casual laugh.

"Getting ready early for trick-or-treaters?" she asked, eyeing his cart brimming with sweets.

"Nah. I've had trouble getting the girls to do their chores, so I figured positive reinforcement might work. You know, get them to brush their teeth, hand them a candy bar—that sort of thing." He cringed. "Not that they'd get to eat it right then, but later."

Josie crossed her arms and pressed her lips.

"What? You think it'd be better if I spanked them?"

"Dallas, most kids want their parents' attention. Have you ever tried something as simple as talking to them— especially Bonnie—and hearing from her why she's developed a penchant for trouble?"

Rolling his eyes, he noted, "I'm a grown man, and if I can't figure out how to fix her, how is she supposed to tell me?"

Hands to her temples, she closed her eyes. "You're an impossible man. Just once, when you ask for advice, and I take time from my schedule to give it, would you at least grant me the courtesy of pretending to listen?"

"I did, but I seriously doubt something as simple as asking Bonnie why she's so sassy is going to produce radical change." Shaking his head and sighing, he muttered, "I'm starting to think maybe you're not such a great teacher."

"Funny," she snipped, "because I'm now certain you're an awful father."

IN THE DRUGSTORE PARKING LOT, Josie was so upset by the nasty exchange that she retched in the grass alongside her car.

Life wasn't just unfair, but downright cruel.

In her heart, she knew she'd been an amazing mother. Emma had been the center of her existence. Josie had been firm when needed, gentle and loving and fun when not. She'd taught her basic numbers in fun ways like lying on the grass, counting clouds.

How dare Dallas accuse her of being anything less than an excellent teacher? Because in doing so, he'd also touched a raw nerve. How many times had she blamed herself for not having been more in tune with her husband? If she'd recognized his drug problem in time to find him help, would her happy life have never changed? Would Emma still be here, a lovely little girl with her whole life ahead of her?

That line of thought sent Josie retching into the bushes.

"Hey…" Tone considerably softer than the last time they'd talked, Dallas stepped up behind her. "You all right?"

"Does it look like it?" she snapped.

"Whoa." Holding up his hands, he said, "I was just asking a simple question. No need to bite my head off."

"Oh—there's every need." She hadn't thought it possible to feel worse, but being near Dallas caused a headache in addition to her nausea. "You and I made a mistake. A horrible, *horrible* mistake. We're not friends.

I don't need you coming over here to check on me, when I'm obviously fine."

"Whatever." Turning his back on her, he walked away. "But I'd do the same for a stranger."

Josie should have been pleased, but was instead oddly sad. Which made no sense. But then neither did this wretched flu refusing her a moment's peace.

"No," Bonnie said that night when Dallas presented her with a new brand of toothpaste.

Betsy announced, "She doesn't like that one, either."

Dallas was on the verge of brushing Bonnie's teeth himself whether she liked it or not, when he thought back to the brief conversation he and Josie had shared before things had gone bad. She'd urged him to talk to his daughters. Genuinely talk to them—as if they were old enough to understand.

"Tell me something," he asked his oldest girl on a whim, "why are you always giving me so much trouble about brushing your teeth? You didn't used to. What's changed?"

Opening her mouth, she put her finger inside, proudly wiggling her right front tooth. "What if when I stick the brush in there it knocks my tooth out and then I choke half to death?"

"Okay, wait—when you threw your last paste in the toilet, you said it was because it tasted bad."

"It did," she said with a cock of her head. "'Cause if it knocked out my tooth and I choked half to death it would've been poison."

Dallas supposed that was logical enough thinking—if

you were five. "So let me get this straight, you refuse to brush until that tooth falls out?"

She nodded.

Betsy suggested, "What if she just brushes all around that one? Would that work, Bonnie?"

"I s'pose." And just like that, the battle and war had been won.

While Dallas was certain this small victory by no means marked the end of his parenting trials, at least he'd managed to do one thing right—and he hadn't even resorted to candy bar bribes.

Though he knew he had Josie to thank, his mouth went dry at the mere thought of admitting her victory. The woman made him crazy. Meaning the less he thought about her, the better off he'd be.

"I'm worried about you." A week later, Josie had just put the last of her kids on the bus when Nat approached, blowing on her hands to ward off the cold. "You're even more pale than usual."

"In case you hadn't noticed," Josie said, hustling into the warm school, "the sun hasn't been out in days."

"Still…" Nat held open the door.

Cheeks stinging from the sudden warmth, Josie asked, "Have I mentioned lately how great you are for my ego?"

"Don't blame me. Shelby and the office crew noticed, too. When was your last physical?"

"Oh, for heaven's sake." Ignoring her friend, Josie headed for her room to work on assembling student portfolios. "When you have something fun to talk about come see me."

Josie had barely been at her desk twenty minutes when her eyelids grew heavy. Exhaustion clung to her, weighing down on her shoulders like a warm velvet cape. Figuring a catnap wouldn't hurt, she rested her head on her desk…

Waking three hours later to find her classroom dark, Josie conceded it was time to give her doctor a call.

BY MONDAY OF THE NEXT WEEK, Josie sat in Doc Haven's office, having her blood pressure taken by his nurse. She still hadn't shaken her bug and it was getting ridiculous how many times she'd had to ask Shelby to watch her class. It couldn't be normal that she spent more time in the bathroom than with her students.

"Perfect," the nurse said. "One-twenty over seventy-five."

"Good to know I'm not having a heart attack," Josie grumbled.

"Oh, now, can't be all that bad. Open up and let me take your temperature." When that turned out to be normal as well, she said, "Run on down to the bathroom and tinkle in a cup for me, and then the doctor will be in."

Josie thanked the woman before completing her task.

Back in the exam room, she sat on the crinkly paper, hating the way it felt beneath her. Adding cranky to her list of symptoms, she slid off the table to fish through a magazine basket. Settling on *People,* she was midway through an article on stars with their own Vegas shows when a knock sounded on the door.

"Everyone decent?" Doc asked, slowly opening the door while reading her chart. Looking up, he seemed surprised. "Well, hello. Don't I usually see you on your turf?"

"Nothing personal," Josie said with a wry smile, "but afraid so. We all appreciated you showing up so fast last week when Lyle Jenkins fell off the monkey bars. From the backward angle of his arm, even I could tell it wasn't a simple strain."

"No kidding," Doc said with a whistle. "Poor kid's gonna be in a cast for a while." Taking a seat on a rolling black stool, he asked, "Back to you, what seems to be the problem?"

Josie described her now-impressive list of symptoms, convinced she must've picked up some rare flu. "I love my job, but it's gotten to the point that I literally have to force myself out of bed in the morning."

"Hmph." Standing, bushy gray eyebrows furrowed, the doctor checked her eyes, nose and throat. He felt the lymph nodes at the base of her head. Had her lie down while he palpated her abdomen and stomach. "All of the usual suspects seem fine. When was your last period?"

"Few weeks ago. It was lighter than usual, but nothing too out of the ordinary."

"Is there a chance you might be pregnant?"

"Absolutely not." While carrying Emma, she'd never felt better. Now, she resembled the walking dead. Whereas she'd been upset with her friends for noticing how awful she looked, now it'd gotten to the point where it wasn't anything she could hide.

Nodding, he jotted the information in her chart. "Sit tight while I get my nurse back in here to draw blood."

Joy. Nothing made her already agitated stomach more uneasy than the sight of her own blood.

Another knock sounded at the door, but instead of the nurse like she'd expected, it was Doc. "Ran into the lab tech in the hall. Looks like we caught a lucky break in figuring out what's wrong."

PREGNANT.

The whole ride home, Josie couldn't decide whether to laugh or cry. Spotting is normal for some women the doctor said when she'd told him about her period. As for her feeling great when carrying Emma, he'd explained that away, too. Apparently each pregnancy plays by its own rules.

In her cozy little house she fed Kitty before making a beeline for Emma's room. While some people went to the cemetery to talk with their deceased loved ones, she'd always felt closer to her daughter here.

"Sweetie, I never saw this coming, did you?"

When she'd heard she was carrying her daughter, she'd cried from happiness. Now, hands covering her still-flat stomach, she wasn't sure what to feel. Of course, she was excited, but in a cautious way. As she would be if it was rumored Santa was bringing her a new laptop for Christmas. No use in celebrating until she had the box—or baby, in this case—in her hands.

On her feet, Josie moved about the room, touching photos of Emma when she'd been a baby and then a toddler and then a little girl at her first teddy bear tea party.

The phone rang.

Josie jogged to her bedroom to answer and said with forced cheer, "Nat, great news. Doc Haven says I'm anemic." True. She wasn't ready to tell anyone the rest.

"That's it? Did you tell him how queasy you've been?"

"He gave me a head-to-toe exam and aside from the iron, I'm the perfect picture of health."

"Whew. That means you'll be able to come Christmas shopping in Tulsa this weekend with me and Shelby."

Laughing, she perched on the side of the bed. "I'm touched by the depth of your concern."

"You know how worried I've been."

"Yes, I do," she said, plucking a brown leaf from the ivy on her nightstand. "I also know how much you've been dreading hitting the malls."

"Got me there," she admitted, "but back to your health, so all you have to do is pop a few vitamins and you'll be fine?"

"Uh-huh." Especially in about seven and a half more months.

When Josie returned the cordless phone to its charger, she was trembling. Not so much from fear of once again becoming a mother, but from telling Dallas he was going to be a father.

Forcing a breath, she dug her cell from the bottom of

her purse and flipped it open to find Dallas's number. Once he answered, she said, "Are you available for dinner tomorrow night? We need to talk."

Chapter Eleven

Dallas was more than a little perplexed by Josie's invitation. Their last conversation wasn't even civil. When he'd questioned her as to why she felt the sudden need to play nice, she'd seemed evasive. Significant? Probably not, but as he parallel parked his truck in front of her vine-covered cottage home, he couldn't help but wonder if there would be more to the night than a simple meal.

Three weeks into October, though it was only six, darkness had fallen on an overcast day. The air was cool and crisp and laced with the scent of burning leaves. Somewhere on the block an old hound bayed. With no leaves on the trees, the lonesome sound echoed down the street.

He liked this season.

Crunching through fallen oak and maple leaves in her yard, he mounted the few steps to the front porch, ringing the bell.

She opened the door, holding out her arm to gesture him inside. "Hurry. It's chilly."

On his way past, he handed her a bottle of merlot and a flower bouquet. "Thanks for the invite."

"You're welcome." She shut the door.

"What smells so good?"

"Roast. It's been in the Crock-Pot all day." He trailed her into a homey kitchen what was too frilly for his taste, but he could see where a woman would find it appealing. While she put the bouquet of fall blooms in an antique Mason jar, he started rummaging through drawers.

"What are you looking for?" she asked.

"Corkscrew." Why, he couldn't say, but his runaway pulse sent signals to his brain that this was a date, when nothing could be farther from the truth. He needed a drink. Preferably bourbon, but in a pinch, vino would do.

From down the hall, a cat came running only to hit a full stop, sitting back on his or her haunches.

"Who is this furry creature joining us for dinner?" Dallas asked, kneeling to stroke Josie's pet behind its ears.

"Kitty is the man of the house, and has highly discriminating tastes. I doubt he would lower himself to sample my fare."

Chuckling, Dallas scratched under the cat's chin. "Sorry, fella. I have a feeling you don't know what you're missing."

"Speaking of missing," she said, nodding behind him. "You might check over there for the corkscrew." Josie placed the flowers on an antique, hardwood table. "Second drawer down, to the right of the stove."

"Thanks."

While he popped the cork, she got glasses, holding them out for him to pour. "You're trembling."

"Hungry," she said, hastily setting them on the counter. "Thomas lost a tooth, then misplaced it. Took a couple hours to find it. My whole afternoon was shot. With what little time was left over, we played number bingo."

"Sounds good to me." He grinned. "Especially since my girls weren't involved in the tooth incident— I hope."

Pushing aside her wine, she said, "You're safe. They actually helped with the search."

"Whew." He feigned wiping sweat from his brow.

"We've got about twenty minutes till the potatoes are ready. What would you like to do? Cards? TV?"

Finishing his wine, pouring a fresh glass, he asked, "How about we use that time to get to the heart of the matter—why you called."

"Yes, um, about that…" Her complexion blazed, much to his dismay, making her all the more attractive. Making the night in general all the more strange.

A timer dinged—saving her from giving him a straight answer.

While Josie took homemade yeast rolls from the oven, she delegated jobs for him like retrieving milk and butter and sour cream that Josie used to create decadent mashed potatoes. Fresh asparagus and gravy rounded out the meal.

Kitty slept through it all, lightly snoring on a thickly padded window seat.

"My mother would be jealous of your skills," he

admitted after dishing out thirds of roast. Creamy horse-radish dipping sauce made his taste buds sing. "At the ranch, she's the only one allowed to prepare meals."

"What did your wife have to say about that?"

"Actually, she enjoyed it. She was a cowgirl through and through. Loved working cattle with me. Hated being indoors." Aside from their love of children, the two women couldn't have been more different.

"Oh." She lowered her gaze to her plate.

"Why would you care? It's not like you and I would ever have a connection that would place you out on the range."

Paling, she excused herself before making a mad dash toward a hall bathroom.

By the time she returned, some of her color was back, but not all. He'd cleared the table and managed to put most of the food away in the Rubbermaid tubs he'd found in a bottom drawer.

"Thanks," she said with an awkward wave toward the nearly clean kitchen.

"Sure. No problem."

She took a Sprite from the fridge, rolling the cool can across her forehead before popping the top.

"You're scaring me," he admitted, alarmed by the way she clung to the counter edge for support.

Waving away his concern, she said, "I'm fine."

At least, Josie's doctor had assured her that physically she and the baby were in tip-top condition. During the first trimester, nausea and exhaustion often came with the territory. But it hadn't with Emma. Which made Josie's predicament all the more confusing. On the one hand, she felt beyond blessed to have been given a second chance at motherhood. On the other, she felt terrified and guilty and shocked. Worse yet, Dallas was an incompetent father.

At least he'd helped with the dishes.

By the time the kitchen was clean, Josie was a nervous wreck. She'd invited Dallas to her home for a very specific reason. One she'd gotten nowhere near broaching.

Mouth dry, she forced breaths, willing her pulse to slow.

No such luck.

Dallas handed her a plate, which, because it was still wet and she was still shaky with nerves, she promptly dropped.

"I'll get it," Dallas said, already on his knees, plucking five clean-cut pieces from the floor and tossing them in the trash. From an undercabinet dispenser, he took a paper towel, dampening it before running it across the floor. "There you go. Safe for your bare feet and Kitty's."

"Thanks. I don't know what's wrong with me. I'm usually not so clumsy."

Back at the sink, washing the gravy pan, he asked, "You ever going to get around to why you're talking to me again?"

"Okay…" Sitting hard on the nearest chair, she sharply exhaled. "You're here for a couple of reasons."

He turned off the faucet.

Seated beside her, he took her hands in his. "Does this have to do with your husband?"

She shook her head.

"Then what? Out with it, already."

Standing, she summoned her every shred of courage to say, "Come on. There's something I want to show you."

Following Josie down the dimly lit hall, the heavy meal Dallas just inhaled threatened to bolt. What the hell had she been hiding?

She stopped before a closed door.

Tears shone in her brown eyes.

One hand to her chest, she used her other to turn a crystal doorknob. The night was moonless. The room black. She fumbled for the overhead light switch. With the room immersed in a soft, golden glow, Dallas lost all words. The scene was reminiscent of the twins' room. Pretty and pink with piles of stuffed animals and a pint-size table set for young ladies and dolls. A canopy bed, dripping in lace, took center stage along with custom-built shelves filled with books and toys and whimsically framed photos. The only thing missing from the enchanted space was the little girl it'd obviously been meant for.

Josie backed into an overstuffed lounge chair, cradling her face in her hands. "Even after four years, the pain feels crushing—like a heart attack no medicine can heal. I wasn't sure if you remembered hearing about the car crash before Hugh's suicide."

Sighing, he perched beside her. "Vaguely, but again, I never connected it with you. Why, Josie, did you feel you needed to hide something like losing a child from me? I mean, I know lately, we haven't exactly been close, but…" Her private pain was none of his business, so why did he feel betrayed? As if her having lost her daughter was a fact he should've known?

"It wasn't that simple." Her expression morphed from grief to all-out rage. "Hugh—he hid an addiction from me. Playing flag football of all things, he tore his rotator cuff. After his surgery, he was supposed to have gotten better, but he was in constant pain. I—I didn't know, but after his prescription pain meds expired, he started buying online. God only knows how many he was taking a day. The night it happened—the accident that took my Emma's life—I had to stay late at school for parent/teacher conferences. I asked Hugh to pick her up from my parents'. On the way home, it started to sleet, and—"

"That's enough," Dallas said, connecting the awful dots. "Bastard. Not that it excuses his actions, but I can see why your husband did what he did." What he couldn't understand was Josie keeping all of this from him. She always seemed as if she had everything together, when obviously, her world hadn't been all sunshine and roses.

Sniffling through tears, Josie nodded, then shook her head. "If I'd kept a closer eye on Hugh… If we'd spent more time as a couple. We had such trouble conceiving. Back then, teaching was a job. Emma was my world. We did everything together. I let Hugh become an afterthought. If only I'd—"

"Stop." He needed time to process all she'd confessed.

Could she have missed warning signs? Though he was hardly in a position to judge, part of him had to wonder how she could have not seen something so horribly broken in a man she'd supposedly loved.

He had to ask, "Is this why the rest of your family moved away? To get a fresh start?"

She nodded. "M-my mother blamed me for what happened to Em and then blamed me again for Hugh. She said horrible things. Called me a pathetic excuse of a mom and wife. As if I hadn't been through enough, her rejection was…unspeakably cruel."

Dallas's heart would've been made of stone if he hadn't felt for her. The woman had been through hell—twice. But why was she sharing all of this now? What was the point? As far as he was concerned, whatever attraction they might've shared was long gone. Their differences were just too great.

He should've gone to her, wrapped his arms around her or kneaded her shoulders, but his feet felt frozen to the floor.

"All of this must seem out of left field," she said, wiping her eyes with a tissue she'd taken from a side table, "but in light of what else I have to tell you, I needed you to understand—everything—that makes me who I am today." Wringing her hands on her lap, she asked, "Remember our night at the bar?"

He damn near choked. "Kinda hard to forget."

"Yes, well, now it will be doubly so. I'm pregnant."

"What?" He knew if he hadn't already been sitting, he would have fallen. This couldn't be happening. Not in light of everything else going on with his girls. Dammit, but he hated himself for being stupid enough to have unprotected sex. For degrading his wife's memory by bringing dishonor on the entire family. Worse still, for putting Josie in an unfathomable position. What the hell was wrong with him? He wasn't eighteen anymore and he sure as hell wasn't in any position to take on a second wife.

"S-say something," she pleaded, looking on the verge of again being sick.

"I want to, but I'm not sure what." He stood and paced, but the room was too cramped for the movement to work off much frustration. "Whereas I presume you've had at least a few days to get used to this idea, you might as well have just hit me over the head with a two-by-four."

Rising, Josie said, "Now that you know, feel free to leave."

He held out his arms only to slap them against his sides. "What do you want from me? An on-the-spot proposal?"

"No, Dallas. You can relax. I don't expect to marry you—ever." Marching to the front door, she opened it for him. "But in the same respect, don't you expect to play a role in my baby's life."

"THAT'S IT, SWEETIE," Natalie soothed, rocking Josie on the foot of her bed while she sobbed, "let it out. I'm sorry I ever pushed that creep on you. I had him all wrong."

"Y-you didn't do anything. I was the one s-stupid enough to sleep with him."

"Yeah, but I did go on about how good-looking he was."

Nodding, Josie mumbled, "But he's not. I hope the baby looks just like me."

"Of course, it will." Nat combed her fingers through her friend's hair.

"A-and I never want to see Dallas again."

"I agree," Nat said with more rocking. "Whatever it takes."

"A-and I need ice cream. Chocolate. Lots and lots."

"Right away." Gathering her purse from where she'd tossed it on the floor, Natalie was instantly on her feet. "You sit tight and I'll be right back with enough sinful calories to keep you and baby happy for weeks to come."

"NOT THAT THIS IS SOMETHING you wanna hear," Cash said after Dallas had told Wyatt and him his news over beers in the ranch's barn office. "But it wasn't too long ago that you were lecturing me about how I owed it to the Buckhorn name to make an honest woman of Wren."

"True," Wyatt said after a swig from his longneck bottle.

"Back off," Dallas warned. "You both know diddly about this situation."

"What's to know?" Wyatt asked. He'd rested his feet on the desk, but drew them down, resting his elbows on his knees. "You got Josie pregnant. She seems nice. *Really* nice. Like a small-town kindergarten teacher should. Now how's it going to look when a few months from now, she starts showing and naming her baby's deadbeat father?"

Slamming the last of his beer, Dallas argued, "Not my concern. I have the girls to consider. They're my top priority."

"This isn't like you." Wyatt's direct stare made Dallas uncomfortable as hell. "What's really the problem? Bobbie Jo?"

"Leave her out of this." Taking another beer from the minifridge, Dallas used the desk's edge to pop the top. "You of all people, have nothing to say on the topic of love."

"He's got you there," Cash chimed in. To Wyatt he noted, "When it comes to the ladies, your track record isn't so hot."

Sighing, Wyatt was out of the chair. "That's it. I've had my daily allotment of you both. I'm out of here." After slapping on his hat, he was gone.

"Feel free to follow," Dallas barked to his little brother.

"Oh—I will. First, you need to ask yourself if Josie's child will mean any less to you than Bonnie or Betsy. If Josie has a son, are you going to give him your name?"

Leaning his head back with a groan, Dallas urged, "Please, leave."

Thankfully, for once in his life Cash did as he was told.

Alone save for racing thoughts and more guilt than a sober man could handle, Dallas reached for a pen and yellow legal pad. He'd always prided himself on his logic. Business sense. What this situation called for was a sound plan.

First, he'd list pros and cons of marrying Josie.

On the pro side, when fire wasn't flashing from her eyes, Dallas liked Josie a lot, as did the girls. Their one time together had been sheer, X-rated fantasy.

In the con column, Josie currently hated him. Thought him an unfit father, which seriously irked the hell out of him. Then there was the not-so-little matter of what went down with her past. Her loss had been tragic, but for Josie's mother to have virtually disowned her, was there truth to the matter of Josie having being negligent by not keeping closer tabs on her husband's drug dependency? If so, what did that say about *her* parenting skills? Was she fit to raise the child they'd created, let alone become a stepmother to Betsy and Bonnie?

A matter Dallas could hardly bear to dwell on were his own unresolved issues with grief. He was apparently well enough for casual sex, but more? A real, lasting marriage took not just love, but a lot of work from both sides. Was he in any way emotionally prepared to offer those things to a woman he hardly knew?

Negatives clearly outweighed positives, but Cash's question wouldn't stop ringing through Dallas's head. Dallas had been man enough to make a child. Was he really prepared to turn his back on the child just because the baby's mother happened to be so wrong for him?

Chapter Twelve

"Come on, guys," Josie urged her students two days later. It was time for them to gather their things to go home. Considering it was Halloween, the day hadn't gone as badly as it could have, but the entire school had seemed especially rambunctious. "Let's hustle."

Watching the Buckhorn twins efficiently fill their backpacks with the day's papers, it occurred to Josie how much they'd grown—at least at school. For the most part, they did their work and conformed to school and classroom rules. As warmly as she felt toward them, she was that perturbed by their horrible father.

Shelby had bus duty, so she stopped by to gather Josie's crew. Next, the children who walked were dismissed, followed by those whose parents picked them up.

Typically, the twins met their father outside, but on this day, they held back, scuffing their sneakers on the hall's tile floors.

"What's up?" Josie asked. "Do we need to call your grandma for a ride?"

"Daddy!" Both girls raced toward Dallas who strode tall and impossibly handsome toward her.

He knelt to scoop them into his arms. "I missed you."

"We missed you, too, Daddy." Betsy squirmed to be let down. "I wanna show you my scary black cat."

"No, me first," Bonnie demanded. "My ghost is *waaay* scarier."

"Tell you what," Dallas said, "while you get them out for me to see, let me talk to Miss Griffin."

"Okay." With both girls momentarily occupied with pilfering through their backpacks, Dallas crammed his hands into his pockets. "Have a second?" he asked Josie.

"Not really." Entering her classroom, she sat behind her desk, moving her mouse to disengage a spook house screen saver.

"Josie," he said in an urgent whisper, "for the other night, I'm sorry. You caught me off guard in more ways than one and—"

"Look, Daddy!" Bonnie held up her ghost. "Isn't he, like, the scariest thing you've ever seen?"

"He sure is."

Betsy pouted. "You don't like my cat?"

"Honey," Dallas assured, "your cat is awfully scary, too."

"Tell you what," Josie suggested, "how about you two take some paper from the special art drawer and make spooky pumpkins, to match?"

"But we're not allowed to *ever* go in that drawer," Betsy reminded.

"True," Josie said, "and I'm proud of you for remembering. But just this once, go ahead."

"Cool!" Bonnie ran in that direction.

"Thanks," Dallas said. "I'd planned a big speech, but…"

"Why are you even here?" she asked, her pain growing exponentially for each minute he was near. "The other night, you pretty much said everything that needed to be said."

"I didn't come close," he admitted. "But like you once told me, we need to talk. Come with the girls and me to the Halloween Festival tonight. We'll make it a no-conflict zone. Maybe we'll figure some things out, maybe we won't, but we owe it to the little guy or gal inside of you to try."

In the worst way, Josie wanted to stick to her guns and deny him, but having always prided herself on putting Emma's needs before her own, Josie knew she'd do the same with this child. Though she had no intention of growing any closer to Dallas than necessary, for the sake of their baby she'd at least be civil.

"Aren't they adorable! Are they twins?" The white-haired woman manning the Weed Gulch Chamber of Commerce's basket-toss booth patted both girls' heads. "I love nothing better on Halloween than Cinderella."

"We're not stupid princesses," Bonnie said, whipping a plastic microphone from her purse. "We're Hannah Montana."

"*Oooh…*"

Dallas apologized to the woman, confessing, "I didn't know who that was, either."

Josie straightened Betsy's blond wig. "You look cute. Just like Hannah."

"Thanks." The girl added lip gloss. "I don't know why nobody knows us."

"They're dumb," Bonnie said.

"That's enough out of you two." Dallas cupped his girls' shoulders, guiding them through the crowd. After stops at more carnival game booths than he cared count, Dallas finally found himself alone with Josie when the girls ran off to a giant, spider-shaped Jupiter Jump.

"Want a Polish sausage?" she asked, nodding toward a stand.

"Sure." He reached for his wallet, but she shook her head. "I don't need your money, Dallas. I'm more than capable of caring for myself and my baby."

"Our baby."

Lips pressed, she graced him with a hard stare before going for their food. With so many issues between them, where did he even start? They'd kept their conversation pleasant around the girls, but now that they were on their own, what would develop?

While she stood in line, Dallas grabbed an empty picnic table.

The Kiwanis sponsored a haunted house, complete with creaking door and cackling witch sound effects and fog rolling out from under the foundation. The home was manufactured and on loan from a Tulsa company that'd set up an adjacent advertising booth.

"Here." Josie set their food in front of Dallas before

straddling the bench across from him. With the girls in view, she said, "I didn't know what you wanted to drink, so I grabbed you a Coke. That okay?"

"Yeah." He bit into his kraut- and onion-covered dog. "Good call. This is delicious."

She nodded. "So? Where do we start?"

"You mean on repairing us?"

"News flash," she said after her latest bite, "but there never was an *us*. We shared a few kisses, secrets and one hot night I'd rather forget."

"Meaning," he asked, "if you had it to do over again, you'd wish you weren't having my baby?" Just asking the question had been surprisingly hard. He wouldn't have expected to even care what she thought on the matter, but inexplicably, he did.

Setting her meal to her paper plate, she molded her hands to her stomach. Was he imagining things, or did the motion produce a wistful smile? She looked beautiful, yet fragile. Her complexion was like porcelain specked with just enough freckles to give her a mischievous smile. At least, what he remembered of her laughing. How long had it been? "No matter how rocky things are between us, I view this child as a blessing."

"On that we agree." If only there wasn't so much more on which they disagreed.

AT HER BALLET CLASS THURSDAY night, Josie felt heavy and awkward and cranky.

Typically, everything from the classical music to camaraderie with her friends boosted her spirits, but tonight, she just wanted to finish already so she could curl up with a good book and a spoon constantly loaded with ice cream.

"This baby kicking your butt?" Shelby asked when class was over. "Last week you looked ready for *Swan Lake* auditions. This week, more like an off-off-Broadway version of *Duck Lake*."

"Ha-ha." Josie knew her friend was teasing, but the words stung all the same. Daubing her sweating chest and forehead with a towel, she admitted, "Last night, I went with Dallas and the twins to the Halloween Festival. On the surface, with the girls, we kept things civil, but an underlying tension ruined the whole night. It's no secret I think he's a horrible father, but what he doesn't get is that beyond that, I deeply resented him for still having his girls, yet botching his duties toward them. Now that I'm pregnant, I feel almost traitorous to Em's memory, like I'm trying to replace her. And along with my second chance, I find myself wondering if Dallas deserves the same. Only we've said such ugly things to each other, I'm not sure if we'll ever be able to take them back. Let alone regain trust."

"Slow down," her friend advised while Josie took off her toe shoes and tucked them into her dance bag. "Everyone at school views you as the most levelheaded, sane one of our bunch. With a baby on the way, the last thing you need is stress. Obviously, if you and Dallas were once hot enough for each other to make this baby, there has to be at least part of a foundation left for you to start building a new friendship."

"I know." Josie slipped on her coat over her leotard and crammed swollen feet into fleece-lined Crocs. "And for the baby's sake, I'm willing to see if I might've judged Dallas too harshly. But what if he doesn't feel the same?"

"JOSIE," DALLAS'S MOTHER said Sunday afternoon, greeting her at the ranch house's front door with a warm smile. "It's so nice to see you again. The girls talk of you all the time."

"In a good way I hope," Josie asked with a cautious smile.

"The best." Taking her coat, the older woman then led her toward a big country kitchen fragrant with lasagna. "I can't tell you how pleased I was when Dallas asked if it would be all right for you to join us for Sunday supper."

"Yes, well…" Josie's stomach lurched. "I was flattered by the invitation."

Friday, when picking the girls up from school, Dallas had confessed his brothers knew she was pregnant, but not his mom. He'd asked her to join him in presenting a united front that they were firm in their decision not to marry, but to jointly raise their son or daughter.

Funny thing is, she had never really agreed to any of that—just took it all in while Dallas outlined his plan as if raising their child meant no more than any ordinary business transaction.

"My son has been acting strangely." Chopping tomatoes for a salad, she asked, "Any chance you know why?"

The back door burst open and in dashed two pink-cheeked energy balls, running to her for hugs. "Miss Griffin!"

While returning their embraces, Josie looked up to see Dallas in all his cowboy glory. No matter their differences, her instinctual, physical attraction to the man was undeniable. Over faded jeans and dusty boots, he wore a long duster, leather work gloves and his hat. His whisker-stubbled cheeks were ruddy from the cold, and when he flashed a cautious smile, his blue eyes shone like the promise of spring. Granted, it might be a long time coming, but in the real sense and metaphorically, she indulged in cautious hope.

"Dinner smells delicious," he said to his mom. To Josie, he said, "Glad you could make it."

"Grandma," Bonnie said, hopping onto a counter bar stool, "I'm hungry. Can I have cookies?"

"No. Dinner's almost ready."

"But I'm hungry now," the girl whined.

"Bonnie…" Dallas warned with a sternness to his tone Josie had never before heard. "How about you and your sister go get Uncle Cash, Robin and Aunt Wren."

"Okay…" Chin drooping, Bonnie held out her hand to Betsy. "Come on, let's go."

Wearing oven mitts, Mrs. Buckhorn noted, "Josie, ever think you'd see the day when Bonnie actually did what she was told with only a minimum of fuss?"

"When it comes to my students, I confess to being an eternal optimist. Both girls are performing much better in class."

Dallas cleared his throat. "While we're on the subject

of kids, Mom, Josie and I find ourselves in a bit of a jam, and—"

"Save it," the eldest Buckhorn snapped to her son, taking the lasagna from the over. "It's no secret Josie's carrying your child. The news is all over town. It's my hope that on the afternoon agenda is damage control? I'll spare you both the lecture on birth control and go straight into asking about the wedding. Because as I've already proven with Cash, there will be a wedding. No grandson or granddaughter of mine will be born without legally taking our name."

More than anything, Josie longed to run off to the nearest bathroom and hide, but that wouldn't solve anything. "Mrs. Buckhorn, this isn't my first time to the so-called rodeo and I don't have the stomach for weathering a second failed relationship."

"Weed Gulch isn't exactly the best place for keeping secrets," Georgina said while buttering French bread, "and I'm also well aware of your past. Trust me, my heart goes out to you for your loss, but that doesn't in any way give you the right to bring my grandchild into the world on a hotbed of scandal. You're a kindergarten teacher, for heaven's sake. What sort of example does it set for our young people when supposed role models are running around town unwed and pregnant?"

"Mom," Dallas said, "that's enough. Josie and I are adults, well aware of the ramifications of our actions."

"Ramify *this,* Mr. Fancy Words, if I have to drag you two down to the courthouse with my own bare hands, you will be married by the time this baby is born."

Chapter Thirteen

"Sorry about all of that," Dallas said to Josie after the longest afternoon on record. In waning sunlight, they stood next to her car. "My mom can be a bit overbearing."

"A bit?" Josie laughed. The light breeze caught her curls, floating them over her face. In that moment, whatever spark had first physically attracted him to her returned tenfold. But no matter how much he wouldn't mind tucking her crazy hair behind her ears, then kissing her until the sun set, he couldn't ignore the bad blood also still simmering between them. "I'm actually a little scared. She does understand that just because the town gossipmongers feel marriage is in our future, it's us who will ultimately decide, right?"

Hands in his pockets both to ward off the chill and to keep from drawing Josie into a reassuring hug, he said, "We'll wait her out. Eventually, she'll get the hint that we control our lives—not her. Trust me, by the time the baby's born, she'll love him or her all the same."

Josie didn't look so sure. "I won't be pressured into anything I'm not ready for."

"You think I would? And lest you've forgotten, before you accused me of being the worst father ever, we used to actually get along. You're the one who started all of our troubles. And for the record, you were also the one spurring us into..." he moved his hands at his hips "...you know."

"That's ridiculous." She raised her chin. "That night was a mutual mistake. You're certifiable," she declared, climbing into her car.

"Ditto."

Watching her drive off until the dust cloud out on the main road faded into rolling hills of winter wheat, Dallas couldn't hide a smile. The woman was infuriating, insulting and downright aggravating. At the same time, she raised his blood pressure to a degree he should've found alarming, but was actually more in the realm of invigorating.

"BONNIE," DALLAS SAID to his daughter after Thanksgiving dinner had been put away. "No matter how many times you ask, my answer's still the same. You're not riding Cookie in this weather."

"But why?"

"Because sleet isn't good for either of you."

Bonnie added hopping to her whines. "I wanna ride my pony."

"She really does," Betsy pointed out.

Josie remained on the fringe of the conversation, drying the turkey roasting pan.

Though Natalie had invited Josie to share the holiday with her family, Josie had thought it best she try making amends with Dallas's mother. Stress was unhealthy for the baby, and no matter how much she wished for the anonymity of living in a giant city where no one gave a flip what she did, the reality of her life was that people were already talking and their whispers hurt.

"You seem awfully quiet." Dallas's sister-in-law Wren nudged Josie's shoulder. "Let me guess, either you have indigestion from too much giblet gravy or you're letting Georgina under your skin."

Wincing, Josie confessed, "I suffer from a little of both."

Forcing a deep breath, Wren said, "Feel free to tell me to butt out, but if you'd like to talk, it wasn't too long ago Cash and I faced the same kind of heat."

"How did you manage?" Josie asked, glad for any advice. "Aside from, well, you know—" she reddened "—Dallas and I are practically strangers. I can't even imagine getting married again. Then there's Dallas himself. Look at him fighting with Bonnie like he's no more mature than her."

"You might want to look again. Since meeting you, he will never admit it, but he's worked hard to get on the right course with his girls."

Dallas had slipped on his duster and now helped Bonnie with her puffy down coat. After tugging on her pink hat, he said, "We'll be right back."

"Where are you going?" Josie asked.

His stare locked with hers. Almost as if he wanted this moment to be about just them, but didn't know how to make it happen. "Bonnie and I had a talk. She's worried Cookie feels bad that she didn't want to ride him on Thanksgiving."

"Yeah," Bonnie chimed in, "but Daddy said if we go visit him and bring him a carrot or apple, he'll still be happy even though he didn't get to ride."

"We compromised," Dallas said with an intensity that left Josie wondering if he'd eavesdropped on her and Wren's conversation.

"I'm glad." When he took both girls by their hands, Josie flashed Dallas a genuine smile. When he returned one of his own, her traitorous stomach flip-flopped. Had she misjudged him? Maybe he wasn't such an awful father, after all?

WITH BETSY ON HER LAP and Bonnie pressed against her with wide-eyed concern, Dallas watched on from just outside the otherwise deserted classroom as Josie said, "Sweetie, I'm sure Thomas didn't mean it. Maybe he's even jealous that you lost a better tooth than him?"

"You think?" Betsy asked.

"He was real mad when my front tooth fell out," Bonnie assured. "Now that yours is out, too, you're gonna be so rich when the Tooth Fairy comes."

Sniffling, Betsy said, "He still didn't have to call me donkey girl."

"I know," Josie assured, smoothing his daughter's long, brown hair. "And if you think about it, he's a silly boy, anyway, because everyone knows donkeys have two gorgeous front teeth."

Eyes wide and looking stricken, Betsy asked, "Does that mean I'm not gorgeous?"

Laughing, giving his daughter an extra squeeze, Josie promised, "You and your sister are the most gorgeous princesses ever. Once Thomas gets a little older, he'd be lucky to have you for a girlfriend."

"Eeuw!" both girls shouted with shrieking giggles.

"I hate boys," Bonnie said.

"Me, too." Betsy nodded.

"What about me?" Dallas asked past the knot in his throat.

"You're not a boy," Betsy giggled. "You're a daddy!"

"Oh, well in that case—" he snatched her from Josie's lap to tickle "—does that mean you'll go on a date with me to get cheeseburgers?"

"Yeah!" Bonnie did her happy dance.

Betsy kissed his cheek. "Can Miss Griffin come?"

"Depends," he said, working to ignore the quickening of his pulse, "did you ask if she wants to go?"

"Do you?" Betsy asked.

Josie's teary-eyed smile rocked him to his core. "I'd love to have cheeseburgers with you—but only if we have onion rings, too."

"Eeeuw," Bonnie said, accompanying Josie to her desk while she grabbed her purse and coat, "I hate those, but Daddy and Uncle Wyatt eat them all the time and then Grandma says they have smelly *unjun* breath."

TWO WEEKS BEFORE Christmas, Natalie sat on Josie's floor in front of a crackling fire. In the winter, they replaced Saturday morning yard sales with scrapbooking and while Nat worked on documenting her summer

Grand Canyon rafting trip, Josie put the final touches on matching minibooks for Dallas's girls.

While Josie changed the TV channel to a home makeover show, Natalie said, "You're getting awfully cozy with the Buckhorn clan. Thought you despised Dallas."

"I do—*did*. Guess he's growing on me. No doubt because his son or daughter's growing in me."

"Rethinking your antimarriage stance?"

"Nope." Back at the card table holding her masterpieces, Josie added snapshots she'd taken of the girls at the Halloween festival, tacking mini foam candy corns to each corner. "For the moment, Dallas and I are back to being friends. That's enough. And the twins are finally settling in. What's it going to do to them if all of a sudden they find out their teacher is carrying their little brother or sister? Talk about freaking them out."

"True." Nat pressed twinkling star stickers over a nighttime campfire shot. "But you're a smart cookie, Josie. So are Dallas's girls. Once you start showing, there are going to be questions you can no longer avoid. Now you're only dealing with the fallout from old biddy gossips. What happens when our school principal and the PTA find out? Dallas's mom was right in that for all of Weed Gulch's so-called advances like the new grocery store and coffeehouse, we still live in a societal vacuum where folks like their pregnant women married."

"Way to ruin an otherwise perfect morning." Josie abandoned her friend in favor of making a run to the kitchen for cocoa with plenty of marshmallows. While waiting for the milk to warm, she stared out the window at the gray day. The only spot of color in the otherwise brown yard was a cardinal looking for food in the empty feeder.

Fear and self-doubt suddenly consumed her.

She couldn't even manage caring for her backyard songbirds; how was she supposed to care for this new baby all on her own? Worse yet, old doubts taunted her with deep-seated fears at the possibility of what had happened with Emma happening all over again. What if that night Josie had been able to prevent Hugh from driving? What if instead of being the good mother she'd thought, in reality, she'd been an accessory to her beautiful daughter's death?

"DADDY, PUH-LEAZE CAN WE SIT on Santa's lap?" Though Bonnie was the one begging, each girl had a deathgrip on his arms. The Saturday before Christmas, Tulsa's Woodland Hills Mall was a mob scene. Santa was apparently a popular guy as the line to visit his workshop wound all the way from JC Penney to Macy's.

"Quit," Dallas barked. "With all the shopping we still have to do, the wait is too long. Besides, if you two pull on me much harder, my arms are going to fall off."

Betsy wasn't buying it. "Miss Griffin, is that true?"

"'Fraid so," she said with a deadpan expression he'd have to thank her for later. "When you're in second grade, you'll learn all about how you have to be careful not to pull fingers, toes or arms too hard. It can be a real problem."

"Whoa…" Wide-eyed, Betsy cupped her hands to Bonnie's ear.

Bonnie whispered back before asking, "If we can't visit Santa, can we have ice cream for lunch?"

Sounded good to him, but lately, whenever he was around Josie, Dallas found himself hyperaware of making the right parental decisions. Her doubting his abilities still irked him and if it was the last thing he did, he'd make her eat her words. He was a good father. Getting better every day. Did he feel one hundred percent confident he was doing the sort of job that would've made Bobbie Jo proud? Not even close. But for the moment, he craved Josie's approval.

"Tell you what," Dallas offered, "how about we have some nice salads. Then maybe fruit for dessert?"

Both girls hung their heads in pouts.

"You know," Josie said, "since it is almost Christmas, it might be a fun tradition to start something silly like rewarding ourselves for being good shoppers by eating an equally silly lunch like nothing but cookies or ice cream."

Dallas argued, "What about the girls getting proper nutritional value?"

Kneeling to give Bonnie and Betsy winks, she said, "That's why God made vitamins, right?"

With both twins smiling, they trekked off to Dillard's to find a gift for Dallas's mother. The jury was still out on what he thought of Josie overriding his healthy lunch plan, but considering he was also in the mood for junk, he'd let it slide.

"Thanks for doing this with me," he said to Josie,

wishing he wasn't loaded like a pack mule with packages. "As you can tell, I need help. Especially with Mom. I always end up getting her a gadget she secretly donates to the annual church yard sale."

The housewares section was not only overwhelming, but dull. China, sheets and pillows. None of which—as much as Dallas loved his mother—he gave a flip about.

"If you check the oil on my car," Josie offered with a playful wink, "I'll tell you what your mom told me she wants."

Grinning, he said, "Done." After trailing her toward sparkling crystal, feeling like the proverbial bull in a china shop, he asked, "Where are the girls?"

Josie nodded toward a bed display where Betsy and Bonnie were pretending to sleep.

"Perfect. With any luck, they'll stay right there until we're done."

She laughed. "No kidding. Maybe you should make a side barter with them?"

Emboldened by her smile, he teased, "A good cowboy's always ready to deal."

"Oh, really?" Her flirty banter reminded him of the days when they'd first met. Seemed like a million years ago. Back then, neither had had doubts about each other, only blazing hot curiosity. "There was once a time when I only liked *bad* cowboys." Her wink stole his breath. Made him crave things he had no business wanting. "Thankfully, I've since learned better."

"Pardon." A sales clerk cleared her throat. "Are those your two little girls?"

Glancing over the woman's left shoulder, Dallas spied his daughters jumping on an expensive-looking bed.

With a mischievous sparkle in her eyes, Josie said to the clerk, "Nope. Those aren't my kids."

"New wine glasses," Dallas's mother exclaimed Christmas morning. "Swarovski crystal even. Dallas, how did you know?"

"I'm that good."

An elbow to his ribs from Josie left him coughing. "They're from me, too."

"Thank you, honey." Georgina waded through the sea of wrappings to give Josie a hug. "I should've known the man who gave me a Halloween-themed scarf last year didn't select a gift this nice on his own."

"Hey," Dallas complained while Wyatt, Cash and Wren laughed at his expense. Robin and Prissy—Wren's Yorkie/Chihuahua mix—slept through the festivities, and the twins were temporarily outside playing with their new bow and arrows. "That scarf was originally a hundred bucks. When I got it for ten, I figured you'd appreciate my finding a bargain."

She grimaced. "Son, you might be my eldest, but when it comes to finesse, you've got a lot to learn."

"Amen," Wren said, seated on the hearth, warming herself by the crackling fire. "He gave me a fruitcake that was harder than any brick. FEMA could use a bunch of them for rebuilding storm-damaged homes."

"Ha, ha, ha." While Dallas pouted, Josie took Wren's gift from under the tree.

Handing it to her, Josie said, "For the record, the

only role Dallas played in this item was surrendering his credit card at the checkout counter."

"I'm intrigued." Wren gave the small box a slight shake, but it made no sound. The wrapping was especially pretty—gold foil with a black velvet bow. "Oh!" Upon opening the even smaller black leather box inside to find a pair of perfectly matched diamond studs, she said, "Dallas, this is too much."

"Considering I never bought you two a wedding gift, and I missed your birthday back in May," Dallas admitted, "I'm hoping those get me back in your good graces."

"Done." Wren hugged her brother-in-law and then approached Josie, but when Josie stood, she touched her forehead and fell back to the sofa.

"Whew."

"Okay?" Wren asked, her voice laced with concern.

Josie nodded. "Just dizzy."

"Did you take your iron tabs?" Dallas asked.

"Yes," she snapped. "Sorry. All of a sudden I'm not feeling so hot." She made a mad dash for the guest bathroom, but unfortunately, Wren, Dallas and his mother were hot on her heels. Once her heavy breakfast came up, her stomach felt better, but her embarrassment level was through the roof.

"Oh, dear," Georgina crooned. Wetting a washcloth, she offered it to Josie. "Should we put off opening the rest of the gifts until after lunch?"

"No," Josie said, relishing the cool fabric against her superheated skin. "Please don't let me ruin your day.

Dallas can run me home and then all of you can finish out the holiday without interruption."

"Nonsense." Georgina turned to her son. "Get Josie a blanket and pillow, then shove your brothers off the long couch and help Josie onto it. A *single* woman in her condition shouldn't spend Christmas alone."

While Dallas did his mother's bidding, Josie remained in the bathroom, rinsing her mouth and trying to get her stomach feeling stable.

With Georgina hollering out the front door for the twins to put coats on or come inside, Wren whispered, "It's okay, you know?"

"For what?"

"To lean on us. Georgina, me—especially Dallas." Hand on Josie's forearm, she continued, "I used to be like you, convinced I could single-handedly take on the world, but ever since figuring out it's more fun to share, I've never been happier."

"Truthfully," Josie said with a slow exhale, "it's not that I'm eager to raise this baby alone, or spend the rest of my days talking to just my cat, but so much more, I'm afraid of everything—loving this child too much. Falling for Dallas only to realize we've made a mistake. In turn, hurting the twins." Hands to her still-spinning head, she fought tears. She'd never been more confused. In the same respect, she had never needed a friend more desperately. Was it possible she could rely on Dallas to help her through not only her pregnancy, but negotiating the treacherous water of being a small-town, unwed mom? "Everything's a mess. My whole life feels upside down."

"I get that. Initially, the only reason Cash and I were together was for our baby. But with time, our relationship grew into more. Now, I can't imagine my life without him."

"I'm happy for you," Josie said, mind swirling with doubts. "But what if Dallas and I never get to that place? What if we were to get together, only he grows to resent me and our baby, instead of loving us? Can't you understand how it would be much simpler leaving well enough alone?"

"Simpler, yes." Wren tidied Josie's hair. "But I guarantee Dallas would be a lot more fun to snuggle with on a cold winter night than your cat."

Chapter Fourteen

"Aside from you getting sick," Dallas said late Christmas night, walking Josie to her front door, "this was a nice day. Good food. Good company—" he gave her a friendly hug "—doesn't get better than this."

"True." Inserting her key in the front door, she said, "I usually spend Christmas with Natalie and her family. They're always welcoming, but then Nat's mother starts lecturing her about how much she'd like grandkids before she turns eighty and next, her dad starts yelling at her mom. Typically, before we've finished breakfast mimosas, Nat's fuming and I'm wishing I could hide in a closet."

Laughing, Dallas knelt to pet Kitty. While he couldn't say they were best buds, at least the cat now tolerated him. "Sounds like you made the right choice in hanging with us. Although we've had our fair share of holiday turmoil. Last year, a little before Christmas, Cash and Wren got married and had Robin all on the same day."

Josie whistled. "I can't top that."

"Wouldn't want you to." Now that Kitty had been properly greeted, Dallas wasn't sure what to do with his hands. He'd liked hugging Josie. Enjoyed the feel of her in his arms, but did she feel the same? How big a dufus would he be if he went in for a smooth move only to have Josie dodge his advances? "On a more serious note, are you feeling better?"

"Much." Was it normal that she seemed fidgety, too? Did she want him to make a move? Even if he did, how far did he go? They might've already gone for a home run, but lately, he felt as if they'd grown to know each other all over again. This time, at a much slower pace.

Deciding to ignore his fears and just go for it, he tenderly drew her against him. When she showed no signs of struggle, he rested his head atop of hers. "Ever notice how we fit? Like puzzle pieces that've been waiting to be put together."

"Read that on a greeting card, cowboy?" The light in her eyes told Dallas she was giving him an old-fashioned ribbing, but in that moment, he wasn't kidding. Yes, he hated the fact that she possibly still didn't think him the most qualified of fathers, but he was getting better every day. By the time his new son or daughter arrived, he'd be the expert all of their kids deserved.

"I'm serious." When she stared up at him, he kissed her. Long and leisurely. Like they had all the time in the world. They'd both learned the hard way that love could be fleeting, but with a little luck and whole lot of prayer, things just might turn out different this time around. "Josie, I'm falling for you."

"I'm not sure how—or even, when—but me, too." After returning his kiss and then some, she admitted, "Since our falling out and then coming back together,

I'm still scared what I'm feeling isn't real. But in the same regard, I can't deny that lately, when we're together, everything's better. Fall colors were more brilliant. Thanksgiving turkey more tender. Christmas lights twinkle brighter."

"Talk about sounding like a greeting card…" Sweeping her jawline with his thumb, he said in an emotion-filled whisper, "That was beautiful. I feel the same."

After more kissing and caressing and sharing feelings with words, they naturally gravitated toward her dark bedroom.

"Sure this is what you want?" she asked, her voice a husky fraction of her normal self.

"Can't you tell?" he asked, pressing her against his swollen need.

"I'm just so unsure—about everything. But most especially, you." As he drew off her blouse and then bra, she shivered.

Stroking the chills from her upper arms, he pulled her into another kiss.

Drawing back only long enough to turn on the bedside lamp, he sat on the edge of the bed, settling his hands low on her hips, pulling her in. With their eyes at the same level, he said, "You're starting to mean the world to me. Sometimes, when I'm alone out on the range, I fantasize about you, me and the girls being a real family."

"I do, too," she said, albeit dropping her gaze. "But…" Her melancholy expression told him she didn't believe him.

Cupping his face, she kissed his forehead and closed

eyes and nose. "I'm scared. All of this has happened so fast. We went from flirting to pregnant to hating each other and now this all in the blink of an eye. It's confusing and exhilarating, yet I don't trust it to be real."

"Me, neither," he confessed, skimming his hands over her full breasts, cupping them, teasing her nipples until she sharply inhaled, burying her hands in his hair. "But at the moment, I'm thinking this is about as real as I can stand without tossing you back on the bed."

"Are cowboys generally this touchy-feely with words?" she teased. "Because as hot as you've made me, I'd prefer less talk and more action."

Shaking his head, Dallas gave the lady what she wanted.

NEW YEAR'S EVE, JOSIE COULD scarcely contain her excitement. With Nat at her house, dressing for the Buckhorns' fancy party, she felt more like they were headed for prom than a ranch.

"I love that," Natalie said, smiling in approval of Josie's silver-sequined cocktail dress.

"Thanks. You're not looking too shabby yourself in that hot little number." Josie's friend rocked a black gown she'd found on a half-off rack at the Tulsa Saks Fifth Avenue.

"Think tonight Dallas will pop the question?" She sat at Josie's vanity table, applying eyeliner.

"Maybe." Josie was on the hunt for the chandelier earrings she rarely had a chance to wear, but loved. "I'm not even sure I want him to. Christmas night, our conversation got pretty heavy. Clearly, neither of us has a clue what we're getting into, but oh, what a delicious way to go."

"You look so happy I'm scared for you. And praying that this time, your fairy tale lasts."

"Don't go there," Josie begged of her friend. "This time around, I'm taking life day by day. No expectations. Just stealing joy where I can. Now, where are they?" It took dumping her jewelry basket on the bed to finally find her earrings. Could Nat be right? Should she be looking for more? Like a lasting relationship with a man whose company she enjoyed?

"Organize your jewelry much?" Glancing over her shoulder at the mess, Nat said, "Relax. No matter what, let's promise to have fun."

Extending her hand for her friend to shake, Josie said, "I'll make that deal under one condition."

After brushing on mascara, Natalie asked, "What's that?"

"I promise to party till dawn if you ask Dallas's brother Wyatt to dance."

"Why would I do that?" she asked with a frown.

"Because he happens to be single and a great guy?"

"I went to elementary, middle and high school with him. Trust me, there's a lot about him you don't know. Plus, he has women falling all over him." After adding bold red lipstick, Nat turned her attention to her nails, adding a clear topcoat. "Besides, I've eaten so many teachers' lounge Christmas cookies that I'm starting to resemble Mrs. Claus."

Josie rolled her eyes. "Who hasn't packed on a few

holiday and/or pregnancy pounds? And as for Wyatt, you going to rely on his past discretions or me? The few times I've met him, not only has he been charming, but there hasn't been a vixen in sight."

"No doubt he hides them in the pool house, fearing his mother's disapproval."

At that, Josie had to laugh. "Trust me, if there's one thing I've learned since Dallas and I have been together, as much as the Buckhorn men love their mother, no matter what she may think, if they see something they want, they'll go for it." Hugging herself to ward off a sudden chill, Josie prayed tonight brought both her and Natalie the happiness they deserved.

JOSIE HAD NEVER SEEN the ranch look more beautiful— or crowded. The Buckhorns were known for hosting a good party and tonight was no exception.

The living-room furniture had been put in storage and in the roomy corner that typically housed Mrs. Buckhorn's rolltop desk, was a five-man swing band. Hundreds of twinkling white lights had been strung from the open rafters and an equal amount of fragrant red roses in silver and crystal vases adorned tables hugging the dance floor's edge. In the dining room was a sumptuous buffet. Waiters roamed, offering champagne and decadent treats from silver trays.

"Whoa," Nat said for only her to hear. "I'm feeling a smidge out of my league."

"Relax," Josie urged. "The whole family is just as gracious as can be."

"Easy for you to say. You're an actual guest. I'm a lowly guest of a guest."

Laughing, Josie took her friend by her hand, leading her to the bar.

Along the way, they encountered Dallas who looked beyond handsome in his tux.

While Nat asked the bartender for champagne, Dallas whispered in Josie's ear, "You look gorgeous and I want to do naughty things with you."

"Sounds good to me." Easing her arm around him, she felt as if they'd known each other years rather than mere months. How they'd gotten so close so fast was a mystery about which she wasn't complaining. "Where are the girls?"

"At Cash's with Mrs. Cahwood. You haven't met her, but she's their housekeeper and sitter." After kissing his date, he added, "Is it wrong that I want tonight to be just about us?"

"Hear me complaining?"

He laughed, then turned to Natalie. "So Josie says I should fix you up with my last single brother."

Choking on a sip of bubbly, Natalie cast Josie an evil glare. "We've, ah, already met and—"

"Come on," he said, guiding her through the still-growing crowd. "Last I saw he was in the den smoking cigars and playing poker, but once he catches sight of you in that dress, I'm sure he won't mind the diversion."

Josie was thrilled that for once her interfering friend was getting a taste of her own medicine.

Nat complained, "I don't even have anything to say."

"You'll figure it out," Dallas assured.

When Natalie glanced back at Josie for help, she just grinned.

"Need me for something?" Wyatt asked upon finding the trio standing beside him.

"No," Dallas said, "but Josie's friend Natalie, here, needs a dance partner."

"Ah, sure." Glancing down at his cards, he said to the six men sharing the table, "Gentlemen, I'm out."

"Come on." Dallas took Josie's arm and practically sprinted out of the den.

"Aren't we going to wait and see what happens?" Josie complained. "I want to know if they hit it off."

"Not to be mean," he said, leading her toward the dance floor, "but I really don't care. My only focus is you. Wanna dance?"

Josie nearly swooned from the intensity of his stare. His white smile. The way his breath smelled of whiskey and that special, indescribable something that her soul recognized as uniquely his.

After slow dancing and fast dancing and laughing more than she could ever remember, Josie was parched. "Whew, I need a break and a drink."

"Both items easily remedied." At the bar, he grabbed two bottled waters.

Striving for a breezy tone, she said, "Next year, I want gallons of champagne."

Kissing her forehead, he said, "Done." Once she'd finished her beverage, he asked, "Want to get out of here for a while?"

"And go where? Last I heard it's eighteen degrees outside."

"Which is why you'll be wearing my coat." Sneaking out the back door, holding Dallas's hand, dressed in the long duster he wore when working cattle, Josie felt as if he were leading her on a grand adventure.

"Where are we going?"

"You'll see…"

Teeth chattering as they struck out down a winding stone trail, she asked, "Is it far? My shoes and swollen feet aren't exactly ideal for late-night hiking."

"Need me to carry you?"

"If you don't mind," she said with a giggle.

Over the crest of a hill was a small log cabin. Candlelight shone through paned windows and sweet wood smoke rose from the stone chimney.

"Here we are." He set her to her feet on the rustic front porch. "This was my great-great-grandparents' home back in the day. It's been updated with luxuries such as plumbing, electric and running water, but otherwise it's pretty much the same."

When he opened the door, Josie couldn't quite believe her eyes. "It's fantastic…"

On the main level was a stone fireplace with flames merrily crackling and stone floor covered in thick throw rugs. A galley kitchen outfitted with a mini-stainless steel stove, fridge and wine cooler. All of the furniture was buttery leather strewn with throw pillows. On an upper level stood a wrought iron bed beside a sunken, glowing hot tub. Through a partially open door she caught a glimpse of a bathroom featuring an oversize, claw-foot tub. Lighting it all were at least a hundred ivory candles.

"My ancestors knew how to live it up."

"I'll say." Warming her hands by the fire, she asked, "Who stays here?"

"Some of Mom's out of town friends. A few East Coast aunts and uncles. Occasionally, folks we've hired to bring out studs or bulls."

"Who lit the fire and candles?"

"I bribed Henry. Wasn't too hard, considering he hates big parties and this gave him an excuse to stay away." On a love seat across from her, he cleared his throat. "Sweetheart, there's a reason I brought you out here." His gaze dropped to his hands. He'd clamped them tight. Was he nervous? If so, why? Her pulse took off on a runaway gallop.

"I-if you're calling it—*us*—quits," she barely managed to get out without crying, "please just go ahead and do it."

"What are you talking about?" he asked with a laugh. "If I were breaking up, would I honestly have bought out all of Dollar General's candles?"

She quivered with relief. With Natalie, she'd put on a brave front, but the more time passed, the more her resolve crumpled. She didn't want to have her baby alone, but with him.

On one knee in front of her, he said, "Enough suspense." From the chest pocket of his tuxedo jacket, he withdrew a gasp-worthy diamond set in platinum. "Josie Griffin, I know this has been kind of a whirlwind thing, but will you marry me?"

Tears started and showed no sign of letting up. Tossing her arms around his dear neck, she hugged him for all she was worth.

"Baby, what's wrong?" Now, he looked even more stressed. "Is this a yes or no?"

"Yes, you silly man. Yes, yes, yes."

"YOU MEAN MISS GRIFFIN is gonna be our mom?" Over her chicken finger kid meal at McGillicutty's steak house in the neighboring town of Lakeside, Bonnie grinned. "Does that mean you have to give me a perfect report card?"

"Bonnie Buckhorn," Dallas snapped, "that's a terrible thing for you to ask."

"Yeah, but, Daddy, you never said if it was true." Betsy had chosen spaghetti and currently wore more than she'd eaten. Josie wiped the girl's face with a napkin.

"For the record," Josie said, cutting into her medium-well filet mignon, "since we're planning a Valentine's Day wedding, we both think it would be best if you two transferred to Mrs. Conklin's room."

"But why?" Bonnie whined. "I *really* love you lots and if you're not around to rescue me, who's gonna save me if I fall?"

"I *really* love you lots, too," Josie said, "but have you ever heard of the big word *unethical*?"

Bonnie shook her head. She wore her long hair in braids and they whacked her ears.

Raising her hand, Betsy wriggled in her chair. "I

know what it is. Uncle Cash drinks *lots* every Friday night."

"That's *alcohol*," Dallas said. "And I'd hardly say one or two beers are overindulging."

"Good guess, sweetie." Josie took another bite of steak. "But in this case, the word means that if I had you and your sister in my class, some of the other moms and dads might say I was treating you better than the other kids."

"But if you love us more," Betsy reasoned, "why is that a bad thing?"

Josie turned to Dallas for help. "Look, ladies, let's say I had one cow I loved more than all of the others."

"You do, Daddy. You named her Lola and she has superlong eyelashes and likes to lick us when we feed her."

"Her tongue is super scratchy," Betsy said with a giggle.

Tossing up his hands, Dallas admitted defeat. "I know—*we* know—switching classes isn't going to be fun, but this is a grown-up thing and you're going to have to trust we know what we're doing."

"You don't." Bonnie sat with her arms crossed and chin hanging low. "I used to really love you, but now I'm mad at both of you."

"That's too bad," Josie said, "because we have more news for you, and this time, it's good."

"Are we going to Disneyworld?" Betsy asked. "I hope so, because more than anything in the whole, wide planet, that's where I want to go."

"Duly noted—" Dallas chewed a bite of his porterhouse "—but tone it down a notch. And, anyway, this is way more exciting than a vacation." Reaching across the table for Josie's hands, he said, "Remember how much fun you two have with Robin? How you think of her like a real-life doll?"

Bonnie dredged a chicken strip in ranch dressing. "Her poop is stinky."

"Yeah," Betsy said, "and she does it a lot."

Josie laughed. "You two are a hoot. You should have your own sideshow."

"What's that?" Betsy nabbed a French fry from her sister's plate.

"Give it back!" Bonnie demanded, snatching it by the portion still dangling from her twin's mouth.

"I hate you!" Betsy declared.

Bonnie stuck out her tongue.

"Break it up." Dallas gave both of them a stern look. Once they'd stopped huffing at each other, he said, "I'd hoped this would be delivered with a lighter mood, but here goes…" Flashing Josie a reassuring smile, he announced, "Surprise! We're having our own baby."

The twins were not amused.

Chapter Fifteen

"Good grief," Josie said across the table, giving Dallas her meanest teacher glare. Under her breath, she scolded, "We talked about your delivery and it was supposed to be sensitive."

"Miss Griffin?" Bonnie asked, "Is there really a baby inside you?"

"Yes, honey, there is. But you know what?"

She shook her head.

"This is scary for your dad and me, too."

Betsy's eyes were huge. "Our mommy died having us. Are you gonna die, too?"

"No," she assured, wishing Dallas would feel free to jump in. "What happened with your mom was a very sad thing, but not everyone who has a baby gets sick."

"Aunt Wren did," Bonnie said. "She had to stay in bed all the time and then we went to see her in the hospital. She looked dead. Like when my frog died."

"That's enough." Dallas signaled to the waiter pushing the dessert trolley. "For the last time, no one's dying."

Betsy started to cry.

"Oh, honey…" Josie welcomed the little girl onto her

lap. "You'll see, once we're a family, and the baby is born all pink and pretty and healthy, we're going to be so happy."

Bonnie crossed her arms. "I don't know if I like this baby."

"Now, you're just being silly," Dallas said. When the waiter finally arrived, he told his daughters, "Pick out some cake or pie. Sugar makes everything better."

"So MUCH FOR MY SUGAR hypothesis," Dallas said after leaving the girls with his mom and then driving Josie home. They sat at her kitchen table eating the chocolate cake they'd had their waiter box to go. "Guess I could've handled that better."

"You think? Your girls are five and everything in their whole world has been turned upside down. Considering how their mom died, they're no doubt shaken by the implications of pregnancy itself, but also losing you to me or the new baby. On top of all of that, they have to change classrooms. They must feel lost."

"Sorry. I promise to from here on out be more sensitive." Dallas helped himself to a glass of milk. He poured her one, too, setting it in front of her. "Drink."

"Way to go on that pledge of sensitivity." She shot a scowl his way, but did follow his suggestion. Finished, she put their cups in the sink and their take-out containers in the trash.

"I could've done that for you."

"Why? I'm perfectly capable."

"That's not the point." Rising to rinse the glasses and

put them in the dishwasher, he said, "In fact, I've been thinking, how about moving out to the ranch before the wedding? That way, you'd have Mom to help cook for you and I can make sure you're taking your vitamins and getting enough rest."

"No." Up from her seat, she went to the living room to see what was on TV.

"Why?" He followed. "It's a perfectly reasonable idea."

"Absolutely not. I have lots to do here before the wedding. And then there's the not-so-small issue of letting the girls slowly adjust to us being a couple. I also need to deal with Em's room." Flipping through channels, she settled on *Iron Chef*. "I want to take my time. Keeping some things out for our baby, storing other items for me to pull out and reminisce over when I'm ninety."

"You're going to be a sexy senior," he crooned, sidling alongside her on the sofa. He never tired of touching her, sharing her warmth. "I totally dig blue hair."

She kissed him. "I'll keep that in mind."

"Want help with Emma's room? Even if I'm just in the house for moral support?"

"Thanks, but I don't think so. You didn't know her."

He wished he had. Didn't that count?

"Please don't take that as a dig. I just mean that it wouldn't have the same impact on you as it's going to on me. It's a task I've already put off for far too long. And if I want to cry or scream at the universe, I don't want you getting concerned."

He sighed. "But as your future husband, isn't it kind of my job to worry about you? Comfort you?" It killed him that on this issue, no matter how hard he might try, there was nothing he could do to help. As a take-charge man, it was inconceivable that there was a problem or pain he couldn't fix.

"Yes," she said, cupping his cheek, "and I love you all the more for feeling that way. Please just try remembering that I had a life before meeting you. Emma… She isn't a loose end to tie, but part of me."

He nodded and understood. And loved Josie all the more for holding strong to her convictions.

"WHO DID THIS?" HANDS ON her hips, Josie surveyed her students, noting that all but a certain two weren't afraid to meet her gaze. Her gorgeous new Coach purse—the one her future mother-in-law had given her for Christmas—had been scribbled on with red, black and green permanent markers. As a teacher, she'd been trained to keep her cool, but this was one time when her patience was sorely tested. "Betsy? Bonnie? Would you please come here."

"We didn't do it, Miss Griffin." Bonnie gave Josie her best wide-eyed innocent look, batting her Buckhorn blues.

"Yeah." Betsy stared at her feet.

"I'm writing both of you passes to go to the office, where I'd like you to tell Principal Moody what you've done."

An hour later, while her students were at lunch, Josie

sat at her desk with a peanut butter and strawberry jam sandwich and milk.

Her classroom door creaked open and in walked Dallas. His scowl told her he was as upset with the girls as she was. "I'll get you a new purse."

Rising, she stepped into his outstretched arms. "I'm not upset about the purse, but how the girls have suddenly regressed. I thought they'd be excited by our wedding and the baby."

"I know." He left her to sit on a pint-size table. "What are we going to do?"

"Nothing we can do other than be patient. I do think it would be best if you officially request to transfer them to Mrs. Conklin's room sooner rather than later, though. It'll give them time to adjust."

"Agreed." Sighing, he swiped his fingers through his hair. "I suppose you think I should be the one to tell them?"

"Until the wedding," she teased with a kiss to his firm lips, "you *are* their primary caregiver."

Groaning, kissing her back, he said, "After that, I'll gladly pass you the disciplinary reins."

"No such luck, stud. I'm afraid that with your new and improved parenting skills, you're in this for life."

"HAVE I MENTIONED HOW EXCITED I am about you officially becoming my daughter?" Georgina Buckhorn had joined her son and Josie and the girls for a Sunday trip to the Tulsa zoo. The day might have been sunny, but blustery wind made it a relief to hide out in the balmy rain forest building.

"Thank you." Josie gave the once-imposing woman a quick hug. "I'm pretty excited to have you for a mother."

While Dallas and the girls ran ahead, looking at exotic fish, monkeys and birds, Josie and Georgina took a more leisurely pace. "It's also an honor you've chosen to marry in the main house. Call me a silly old woman, but to have all of my children's weddings there would be…" As her words trailed off, Josie wondered if she was thinking of Dallas's runaway sister, Daisy.

"It won't hurt my feelings if you'd rather not talk about it, but have you tried looking for your daughter?"

"Gracious, yes," she said in front of the anaconda. "When she first left, we had a P.I. searching full-time. He explained that if a person wants to vanish, it's really not that hard—especially if they're off the so-called grid. Once she turned eighteen, with the entirety of her trust fund at her disposal, there's no telling what she did. The man's still on retainer and every so often calls to tell me he's checked out another dead-end lead."

"I'm sorry."

"Me, too," she said with a resolute nod. "It kills me, knowing she's out there, but wants nothing to do with us. I can't fathom what drove her to such an extreme."

From farther down the trail came a familiar voice issuing a Tarzan jungle call.

"Oh, dear…" Georgina gritted her teeth. "Looks like one of my darlings is in trouble again."

After hustling in that direction, Josie was appalled to find Bonnie swinging from a vine hanging at least ten feet over where they stood.

"Look, everybody! I'm Jungle Girl!"

"You're Grounded Girl," Dallas scolded. "Get your behind down from there."

A zookeeper came running. "Sir, we have strict rules about that sort of thing."

"I know." Turning to Josie, he asked, "What do I do?"

"Knock her down with a spear," Betsy suggested. "I told her not to be climbing."

Hands on her hips, Josie said, "Bonnie Buckhorn, scoot right back the way you came. That vine is for monkeys—not you."

Bonnie stuck out her tongue. "You're not my mom or my teacher. You can't tell me what to do."

The zookeeper momentarily vanished only to return with a ladder. As if he'd had prior experience at this sort of thing, the man calmly scaled to Bonnie's height and plucked her down.

"Thank you," Georgina said, reaching into her oversize leather purse. "Are you allowed to accept tips?"

"No." He folded the ladder. "But I'm afraid per zoo rules I'm required to ask you to leave."

Betsy crushed Bonnie's toes with the heel of her sneaker. "Thanks a lot, monkey brain."

"You're a monkey brain!"

Dallas sighed. "So much for our big day of family fun." Just when he'd thought he had everything together, why did he now again feel as if he was letting his girls and Josie down? Where were the manuals covering what to do when your kid goes nuts at the zoo? Had he been premature in proposing? If he couldn't handle his kids, how would he cope with yet another child and wife?

"IT'S PERFECT," JOSIE SAID, gazing at the dreamy white wedding gown in Special Day Bridal Shop's octagonal mirror. "Think it'll still fit in another three weeks?"

Natalie cocked her head sideways. "From this angle, it looks like there's room to spare in the waist. And surely to goodness you're not going to put on that much weight before the wedding."

"It's ugly." Bonnie stopped twirling in her purple bridesmaid dress just long enough to cast Josie a mean look.

"I think so, too," Betsy chimed in.

With a knot in her throat, Josie made it to a count of five in her head, but Nat beat her to the punch.

"Why did you say that?" Natalie asked the girls.

Bonnie pressed her lips tight and crossed her arms.

Betsy resumed twirling.

"Conference time," Josie said to her future stepdaughters. Hands on their respective shoulders, she marched them to the nearest chair. "Bonnie, we're going to talk first. Remember when you used to sit on my lap and give me your best hugs? I thought we were friends?"

The girl didn't say a word.

"And, Betsy," Josie continued, "you once told me I was not only the best teacher, but the best movie friend ever. What's happened for you two to suddenly be so mean?"

"Are you upset about the wedding or the baby?" the school counselor in Natalie asked.

"I hate that baby," Bonnie said. "It's not gonna be cute like Robin. We're gonna have a ugly baby."

Tears sprang to Josie's eyes and she was dubious as to whether she'd be able to hold them at bay. She knew the girls—Bonnie especially—were just acting out over hurt feelings. They were not only upset about having to change classrooms, but no doubt about how much time Josie had spent with Dallas and their grandmother in planning the wedding.

"Bonnie Buckhorn," Nat scolded, "you should have your mouth washed out with soap."

"If you did that," the girl said, raising her chin, "I'll tell Daddy and he'll ride his horse over you."

Hands covering the tears on her cheeks, Josie asked her friend, "Please help me get out of this dress. I think it's best we go."

FRIDAY NIGHT, WITH THE GIRLS at a sleepover, Dallas lounged with his future bride in the ranch's guest cabin. They'd just finished practicing for their honeymoon and if practice made perfect, they'd have an awesome time. "Sure you can't get in the hot tub? It looks inviting."

"I know…" She rested her cheek against his chest. "I can take regular baths, but all of my pregnancy books say spas aren't a good idea."

"Fine," he said with a slow, sexy grin. "Be a party pooper."

"Listen here, cowboy, if we *partied* much harder, this antique bed would break."

"Excuses, excuses." Gliding his hand up and down her back, he said, "I keep forgetting to mention it, but

Mom's been nagging me to ask you what's going on with the girls' dresses. She said you'd know what that means."

Groaning, holding the sheet to her chest, Josie sat up in the bed. "I didn't want to bother you with this, but the girls, Nat and I had an incident at the bridal store."

"Oh?" Eyebrows raised, he asked, "Bonnie didn't knock over any racks or climb a rentable trellis, did she?"

With a halfhearted laugh, she said, "I wish that was all she did." Relaying the hurtful things the girl had said, Dallas watched helplessly as Josie's eyes welled with tears.

Trying to be practical, he edged closer to her. "Sure those were her exact words? Maybe you heard wrong? I can't imagine my Bonnie being that deliberately cruel."

She snorted. "You also couldn't imagine her smashing cake in a boy's hair, either."

"That was ancient history. Bonnie's matured a lot since then."

"I agree." Josie scooted away from him and off the bed, in the process, treating him to a magnificent view. Her belly was just starting to curve outward and the sight never failed to stir him both on an emotional level and a little further down. "But lately, she's backsliding."

"Agreed. I promise, I'll talk to her. But you need to give her time. She's a kid. Don't rug rats need extra space to adjust to big life changes?"

In the bathroom, she turned on the shower.

"Want me to get in with you?"

When she didn't answer, Dallas took it as a bad sign.

Resting his hands behind his head, it dawned on him that if kid angst was the toughest hurdle they'd have to face, they'd be lucky. Five minutes passed. With the water turned off and Josie standing on the bath mat, wearing nothing but water drops, he asked, "How's the house packing going?"

"So-so." Was it wrong of him that he loved watching her pull on silky panties almost as much as watching her take them off? "I went ahead and called the Realtor you recommended. The asking price she suggested was more than I'd expected in this market."

"That's good." Holding out his arms, he said, "Come here so I can kiss the baby."

She indulged him, but didn't look happy about it. "I think the baby's had enough attention. Remember how we're supposed to be planning a menu and looking through bridal magazines for floral ideas?"

Wearing nothing but a hopeful smile, Dallas patted the empty space on the bed next to him. "By now you should know I do my best work between the sheets."

TUESDAY AFTERNOON, JOSIE WAITED in front of the school with the twins for their father. They were all going to taste wedding cake samples and then make their final selection. She and Dallas hoped that by including the girls in every aspect of the festivities that they might be more accepting of the change still to come. Alas, so far, their plan hadn't worked.

"I'm hungry," Betsy complained.

"I'm cold." Bonnie wriggled in an attempt to look as if she were shivering.

"Your dad will be here soon," Josie said to Bonnie, hugging her for added warmth.

As if Josie had the dreaded cooties, Bonnie lurched away.

To Betsy, Josie said, "You'll be eating lots of cake in only a few minutes."

"That's too long. I'm going to starve half to death."

"Yeah," Bonnie said, "Betsy's gonna starve and it's gonna be all you and your baby's big, fat fault."

The force of the girl's anger struck Josie like a punch. How long were the twins going to keep this up?

Thankfully, Josie's parental back-up finally arrived.

"Daddy!" All smiles, Betsy and Bonnie ran to the truck.

At a more sedate pace that would hopefully allow her to sneak in a few deep, calming breaths, Josie followed.

"Hi," she said, climbing onto the front seat next to Dallas. Before fastening her seat belt, she leaned over for a kiss.

"Hey, girls," he said to the backseat crew. "Have a fun day?"

"No," Bonnie snapped. "I'm hungry and Miss Griffin said I don't get to eat."

"Daddy," Betsy said in her best woe-is-me tone, "why does Miss Griffin hate us?"

"Oh, for heaven's sake," Josie couldn't keep from exclaiming. "You two know how much I love you, but that doesn't mean I'm not going to do everything in my power to help you grow into responsible and respectful young ladies. Dallas, pull over. We all need to talk."

"Something going on I'm not aware of?"

"Plenty." As she filled him in, Dallas's expression grew ever darker.

Parking on the shoulder of the cake lady's dirt road, he turned off the truck, unbuckled his seat belt, then turned around to face the girls. "Out with it. What's the problem? I know you both love Josie. Why are you treating her this way?"

Neither of them said a word.

Josie sucked in a deep breath. "You two don't know this, but I used to have a little girl. Her name was Emma and I loved her so much it hurt."

"Where is she?" Betsy whispered.

"In heaven," Josie managed. "I'm not telling you this to make you sad, but to let you know I understand about hurting and being confused and sad and angry all at the same time. I know how much you love your dad, and I promise—" she crossed her heart "—I will never, ever take him from you. All I want is for you two to give me and this new baby a place in your family. It's been a long time since I've had a family and more than anything, I could really use one."

Bonnie said, "But I'm scared if we give you and that baby our daddy, we won't have one."

"Yeah." Betsy nodded.

Dallas sighed. "What do I have to do to prove to you guys that just because Josie and the baby are now going to be part of our lives, that nothing's really going to change? We'll live in the same house. Go to the same places. Watch the same TV shows. Not only will you still have me and Grandma and Henry and Uncle Cash and Aunt Wren and Robin and Uncle Wyatt to love, but Josie and a new baby brother or sister. No one's taking love away from you, only giving you more."

"Oh." Now Bonnie began to cry. Unbuckling her seat belt, she scrambled over the seat to sit on Dallas's lap.

Betsy did the same, only clinging to Josie.

"How great is this?" Dallas asked, rubbing his daughter's back. "Now, you all don't even have to share laps."

As much as Josie appreciated the current calm, she couldn't help but wonder if this was but their first family storm.

Chapter Sixteen

"What a relief that for the moment, anyway, everything's worked out." Standing on one of the kitchen-table chairs, Natalie took a vase from an upper cabinet. Josie had offered to spring for pizza if Nat helped organize for the big garage sale she was holding that weekend. "Do you think from here on out, the girls will behave?"

"I hope so. I don't blame them for being jarred by all of this. I'm a grown woman and it's still taking me a while to adjust."

"After the wedding," Nat said while washing dust from a waffle iron Josie hadn't used in years, "things will get better."

"From your lips to God's ears."

After Natalie left, the remaining mess was overwhelming. Knowing the only sane portion of the house was Emma's room, Josie shuffled past boxes and packing wrap and tape to the one place she'd always felt surprisingly strong. As if her daughter watched over her, assuring her, *Everything's going to be all right, Mommy.*

For the longest time, Josie sat in her favorite chair,

eyes closed, imagining the feel of Emma on her lap while reading a bedtime story. She'd smelled so good. Like sweet baby curls infused with her favorite strawberry shampoo.

They'd played the little piggy game with her chubby toes. Sang silly songs and tickled and giggled and talked of handsome princes and princesses and happy kingdoms where everyone smiled all the time.

Without realizing it, Josie had begun to cry.

Rather than drying her tears, she wore them as badges of honor. She carefully gathered tissue paper and special-bought plastic bins. One by one, she took tiny dresses from tiny hangers. She smelled them, caressed them, held them to her nose for just one imaginary trace of her little girl's essence. And then she neatly folded them. Wrapped them in pink tissue. Kissing each one before putting it away.

Part of her very much wanted another girl.

Another part feared she couldn't bear it.

SATURDAY MORNING, THOUGH the temperature was a chilly fifty, with no wind and plenty of sun, the day promised to be perfect for the liquidation of Josie's former life.

"Where do you want your tables set up?" Dallas asked with forced cheer. Though he had ranch duties to perform, he'd volunteered to come by early to help.

She pointed to either side of her driveway, while across the garage opening, she strung a line from which to hang clothes.

It was only seven in the morning, but already a few

folks with big trucks and, she suspected, flea market booths had stopped by to rummage through items she had yet to set out. With the pending move, she'd taken to parking on the street, using her garage for box storage. She'd finished the painful process of sorting Emma's things and had donated a box of clothes to a nearby town's women and children's shelter. For treasured items such as stuffed animals that held special meaning and Emma's cherished sterling silver tea seat, she'd wrapped them in tissue and placed them in extra-sturdy plastic bins.

Betsy and Bonnie were inside on her sofa, groggily watching cartoons and eating donuts.

With her sweet house nearly empty and the yard sale assembled, Josie sat in a lawn chair and finally allowed the finality of what she was doing to sink in.

"We okay?" Dallas set up a chair next to her.

Swallowing the lump in her throat, she admitted, "I'm scared. Most everything I own is out here on the lawn."

"I can see where it must be upsetting, but—" he took her hands, eased his fingers between hers and raised them to his mouth to kiss "—once you get past this, you'll never look back. We're going to lead a great life."

Promise?

As the day wore on, so did Josie's exhaustion.

The girls grew bored in the house and they were now pretending to be storekeepers with the crowd.

"This clock thingee's dirt cheap," Bonnie said to a

woman wearing Coke-bottle glasses and a crooked red wig.

"Thank you, doll," the woman said, "but I don't need one of those."

"What do you need?" Betsy asked. "Betcha we got it."

The shopper patted each girl's head before fishing through a ragged coin purse. "Here you go," she said, giving them each a penny. "Buy yourself some nice candy."

The girls looked unsure as to where they'd buy candy that cheap, but thanked the woman anyway. Watching, Josie and Dallas shared a laugh.

The day wore on.

Dallas brought them all sub sandwiches and chips for lunch.

Georgina stopped by and purchased a well-read copy of *Wuthering Heights*. "I loaned mine out years ago and never got it back," she explained, giving Josie a quarter.

"I wanna quarter," Bonnie demanded, holding out her hand. "We're making deals."

"If you want money," Georgina explained, "you have to sell me something. What do you have that I might be interested in?"

Betsy tugged her grandmother by her hand toward a pile of movies and CDs. "I think you'd *looove* this." She held one of Hugh's old slasher movies.

"Do you have anything more scary?"

Considering the bloody cover, Betsy was again looking confused.

By day's end, most everything was gone. Josie's furniture and dishes and small appliances. Collectibles that didn't mean all that much and movies she never watched. Electronic gadgets she rarely used.

After the wedding, she'd move into Dallas's room at the ranch. He had promised, however, to clear out more than half of the walk-in closet. He'd also assured her there would be plenty of well-ventilated attic space for Emma's things or anything else she wanted to store. As for her framed pictures and favorite mementos, Josie was given free rein from Georgina to scatter them amongst the rest of the family photos. After all, the ranch was to be her and the baby's home, too.

"Want me to start boxing the rest of this for donation?" Dallas asked after a big yawn.

"Sure." She gathered the last of the clothes from the line, placing them in a pile. The knot that had held the rope in place was tight, but by standing on a paint can, she managed to work it free.

Stepping behind her, Dallas barked, "Get down from there. What if you fell?"

"See…" Once down, she performed an elegant pirouette. "I'm still in perfect working order."

Hands on her hips, he knelt to talk to her tummy. "Baby, are you hearing the amount of sass your father has to put up with?"

"Yeah," she retorted, "and if you don't help me finish so the baby and I can eat, you're really going to feel my wrath."

"Remind me next time you see Doc that he needs to give you anticranky pills."

With all of the leftover items boxed and in the back of Dallas's truck, they went inside for the girls, who lounged in front of the TV.

"Ready to eat?" Dallas asked.

"Only if we get ice cream," Betsy said.

"News flash," her father announced, "you're going to get what you get and not pitch a fit."

Bonnie rolled her eyes.

"Go ahead." With everyone else on the porch, Josie held back. "I'll lock up and close the garage door on my way out."

Dallas waved acknowledgment.

Kitty sat in the middle of the kitchen floor looking mighty perturbed at the change in scenery. At least his window seat cushion hadn't been sold. He, too, would be making the move to the ranch, but Josie worried he'd spend half of his life under beds and the other half under sofas.

With the space empty, the garage had taken on a lonely feel. Josie told herself she wouldn't get melancholy about selling her home, but that was easier said than done. After pressing the door's button, she made a mad dash to get out, feeling like Indiana Jones easing under just in time.

Only outside did it dawn on her that the garage was too empty. She'd had two plastic tubs filled with Emma's favorite toys, and two more with clothes to be worn by the baby. Had Dallas carried them inside for safekeeping?

She punched in the code for the door to open.

Sure enough, the items weren't where she'd put them.

Trying not to panic, she performed a room-by-room search, but still came up empty-handed.

Running out to the truck, she asked Dallas, "What happened to Emma's things?"

"I never touched them. As far as I know, they're still where you set them."

"Oh, God." Hands over her mouth, nausea struck with a vengeance. Racing to the evergreen bushes ringing the porch, up came lunch. The contents of those boxes were all that remained of her precious daughter.

"Relax," Dallas said, rubbing Josie's shoulders, "they've got to be here somewhere. Stay out here with the girls and I'll look."

He returned, shaking his head. "Let me call Mom. Maybe she remembers something."

Throughout the brief conversation, Josie fought for air.

Dallas finally ended the call, only to pull her into a hug. "Honey, I'm so sorry."

"For what?" she practically shrieked. "What did your mom say?"

Lips pressed into a tight line, he glanced across the yard to his truck, to the two girls chatting up a storm in the backseat. "When you and I were helping that couple who bought your entertainment center, Mom saw Betsy and Bonnie tell a man he could have all four boxes for five dollars. Mom remembers because she made a point of asking the girls if the items were supposed to have even been in the sale."

"No…" Josie whispered with sorrow stemming from deep in her soul. "Please, no."

"I'm sorry." Dallas held her through her tears. "Is there anything I can do to help? Name it. Hell, we'll book a private jet to Paris if that would in any way make up for what the girls have done."

Chilled and angry and hurting, she snapped, "What I want are my child's belongings to have not been carted away in a yard sale. What I want is for you to ground those two for the rest of their little lives."

"Josie, I know you're hurting, but the girls didn't mean it. They assumed anything in the garage was fair game to sell. They were trying to help."

Dallas might have been saying one thing, but all she heard was: *no matter how badly my daughters hurt you, they will always come first.*

"How do I forgive them?" Josie asked Nat during a commercial break from their favorite reality show. With only two weeks until the wedding, Josie's friend had invited her to live in her guest room now that her house no longer felt like home.

Kitty, still full from his dinner, had curled into a ball in Natalie's scrapbooking box.

Muting the TV, her friend said, "Wish I had an answer for you. For years, I've prayed you'd stop putting so much emotional stock in Em's things. Now, I get the feeling you're mourning her all over again."

Unable to speak past the knot in her throat, Josie nodded.

"I was so sure marrying Dallas was right. Now, I've never been more uncertain. Even worse, the Realtor came by school this afternoon with a full-price offer on my house."

"Why didn't you tell me?" Nat asked. "We should've gone out to celebrate."

"How can I be happy about a transaction I'm no longer sure I want?" Playing with a throw pillow's fringe, Josie knew Dallas was the one she should be talking to, but how could she when she was having such doubts?

"Worst-case scenario, you move in with me until we find you a new place. But please don't do anything drastic. There's no way Bonnie and Betsy could've known how much the contents of those boxes meant."

"I know." Cupping her newly rounded belly, Josie prayed for answers. Why did her dream now feel like a nightmare? As if her life's foundation had been ripped out from under her. "But that does nothing to ease my pain. I feel raw inside."

"When's the last time you talked to Dallas?"

The teapot whistled on the stove.

"He called while the kids were at morning recess." Josie headed for Nat's efficiency kitchen to make a cup of orange spice.

"Did you have a good conversation?" Natalie asked beside her, reaching in a cabinet for graham crackers.

"Not really. We ran over a few items for the wedding. That's it." The tea scalded Josie's tongue. Wasn't it just her luck that while she'd been aiming for something nice and soothing, she'd only wound up more annoyed?

"Want my advice, you—"

"Not really." Josie forced a grin.

"Ha-ha. Call him. Now. Even if you all just hit the Waffle Hut out by the toll road for a late-night snack, it'll be good for you to talk."

"I'M GLAD YOU CALLED," Dallas said, taking Josie's hands across the Waffle Hut's booth table. "I hated how we left things Saturday."

"Me, too." She looked as beautiful as ever, but fragile, with dark circles under her eyes.

"Getting adequate sleep?"

She shook her head. "Too much on my mind. Plus, Nat's guest mattress has more lumps than her disgusting mashed potatoes."

He winced. "You're welcome to stay in our guest cabin. It's impossible to not get a good night's rest out there."

"Thank you. I would, but I don't want the girls getting any more confused. I thought our marriage would help them, but I'm afraid it's only going to hurt."

"Help them with what?" he asked after a waitress took their order. "They've got everything kids could ever want or need. You and I both have been spending more time with them than ever."

"True." Her usually bright complexion was sallow. Her tone dull, as if she'd rather be anywhere on earth than out to eat with him. Though her stomach had swelled, the rest of her appeared gaunt.

Leaning forward, he said, "Be straight with me, Josie. Do you still want to get married?"

After a pause, she said, "Of course." Giving his hands an extra-strong squeeze, she added, "But everything's changing too fast. First, my body. Now, my house. Emma's things being sold off for practically nothing to a flea-market dealer. I know what happened was an accident, but I can't get past how badly I want my daughter back." She'd choked on her last words and tears streamed her cheeks. "I'm swimming with nowhere to get out of the water."

"Sweetheart..." he left his side of the booth to join Josie, pulling her into a hug. "That's just it. Emma will always be with you. In your heart. You don't need dresses or books or a tea set to remind you. All you need is to close your eyes and remember." Stroking the tops of her fingers with his thumbs, he said, "If that doesn't work, lean on me. When are you going to learn that no matter what, I'm here for you. But I'm not psychic. You have to ask. Tell me exactly what you need whether it's a late-night cheeseburger or strong shoulder to cry on."

Nodding, her teary-eyed expression struck him as alarmingly hollow.

"What does Natalie say about all of this? She's the school counselor, right?"

"I'm pretty sure she thinks I'm going off the deep end."

"Nah." He smiled. "You're just understandably tired from lugging around my big, strapping son."

Ignoring his stab at humor, she asked, "Please take me home with you. Maybe I could sleep if you'd hold me."

"Done. How about we get our food to go, and you can eat in a nice, warm bath. Sound good?"

"Like heaven."

Thirty minutes later, Dallas had helped Josie off with her clothes and settled her in the water. He assembled her meal on a plate, nuked it for a minute and then set it on the stainless steel toiletry rack suspended across the tub.

"Need anything else?"

Upon taking her first bite, ketchup dribbled on her left breast. "Napkin, please."

Grinning, he leaned close, lapping up the mess.

"Mmm." Closing her eyes, she finally gave him the satisfied smile he'd been craving.

He took the burger from her, stealing a bite for himself. When more ketchup fell, he licked that, too.

"You did that on purpose, didn't you?"

"I'll never tell."

Holding out her arms, she commanded, "Leave the food alone and get in with me."

"Thought you'd never ask."

After making awkward, splashing, laughing love, Dallas added more hot water and then took the fancy spa shampoo his mom had placed in a basket and poured some into his palm. He warmed it, then with Josie leaning against his chest, massaged it into her scalp. Her hair was one of his favorite things about her. It was long and vibrant and unpredictable—just like her.

"Feel good?" he asked when she groaned.

"Indescribably so. You might want to ration this spoiling or I'll be expecting first-class service every night."

"I'm sure we can work out a deal," he said in a suggestive tone.

"YOU LOOK PRETTY," SHELBY mentioned as they moved through Wednesday's lunch line. It was pizza day and both craved junk food.

"Thanks. I feel pretty—and hungry." When it was her turn in line, she asked Paula for two slices.

"How's the wedding planning business?" her friend asked on the way to the teachers' table. "You're down to what? Only a week and a few days?"

"Don't remind me." Seeing Shelby struggle with her milk carton, she opened it for her.

"You have ninja skills when it comes to opening these things."

Josie teased, "That's why I make the big bucks."

As more friends joined their table, conversation ebbed and flowed. Josie glanced across the cafeteria to see Bonnie and Betsy bathed in midday sun. They were laughing with the girls in their new class and looking adorable with the braids she'd made for them that morning. They didn't know she and their father had spent the night together in the guest house, just that she'd decided to join them for breakfast. Their actions still stung. Josie wanted to forgive them for selling Emma's belongings. It had been an accident. Her brain understood, but her heart hadn't gotten the memo.

She and Dallas had made love that morning. Slow and sweet and tender, Dallas had shown her in fifty little ways how much he cared. Her worries about marrying him should have vanished. Instead, the knot in her throat felt like a grapefruit.

Chapter Seventeen

"Surprise!"

When Josie walked into the dark school gym hand-in-hand with Dallas, the shock of encountering at least a hundred friends all assembled for what was supposed to have been a low-key bridal shower was enough to send her pulse racing.

"Did you know about this?" she asked.

"Nope." Wearing a big grin, he indeed looked as stunned—and flattered—as she was.

A DJ played a rock-and-roll version of the wedding march while friends and coworkers crushed them with well wishes. The normally utilitarian space had been transformed into a Valentine wonderland. Round tables dotted the room and the wood floor had been covered in rose petals. It took three tables to hold all of the gifts and another long table bowed from the weight of appetizers, punch, candy and cake. Foil red and pink hearts hung from the ceiling along with plenty of red streamers.

The cake was a work of art shaped like an old-fashioned red schoolhouse complete with a candy playground, students, a teacher and of course, a cowboy.

Bonnie and Betsy ran up to their father. Their grandmother grabbed hold of their hands, trying to slow them down.

"Are all of those presents for me?" Bonnie asked, gaping at the colorful pile.

"They're for Josie," Dallas said. "This is her bridal shower. One day when you and Betsy get married, you'll have a party like this, too."

"Do I have to marry a boy?" Betsy asked. "I want the presents, but no kissing."

Laughing, Dallas seized the moment to lay one on his glowing bride-to-be.

Shelby handed Josie a glass filled with red punch. "Considering the theme, we should have warned you not to wear white."

"I'll be careful," Josie assured. Though her white, cashmere sweater was a favorite of her few new maternity clothes, she was also parched. The ginger ale-cherry blend hit the spot.

"We've got great friends," Dallas noted, nodding across the dance floor at Henry and their neighbor Dorothy boogying with the twins.

Snuggling against him, Josie couldn't have agreed more.

After everyone had worn themselves out from doing the Chicken Dance, eating and getting their entries ready for the toilet paper wedding dress contest, it was time for gifts.

Bonnie and Betsy didn't even try hiding their displeasure at not receiving a single thing. While most guests oohed and clapped for everything from an exquisite vase to sumptuous lingerie, the twins sat in a corner with crossed arms and scowls.

Finally, Dallas headed over to talk to them.

Josie wasn't sure what he'd said, but a few minutes later, the girls were running and laughing with the few other kids and politely asking for seconds on cake.

Wonder of wonders, Dallas was turning into a surprisingly good father.

THE REHEARSAL DINNER was being held poolside, and through the magic of lots of money and Georgina's considerable party-planning skills, she'd rigged a heated tent over the pool deck, completing the scene with floating candles and fake floating swans. She'd fought for real birds, but Dallas had convinced her that if they paddled into flames it could result in adding them charbroiled to the menu.

"Georgina," Wren said, "you've outdone yourself. I've never seen the house look more beautiful."

"Thank you." Dallas's mother beamed. "I can't claim all the credit, though. My new daughter-in-law is no slouch when it comes to planning."

"You're being overly gracious," Josie said. "All I remember saying is I love a good filet mignon and you took it from there."

Adjusting an off-center floral arrangement, she said, "Every party has to start somewhere."

A jazz singer crooned Dean Martin favorites while a chef created flaming shrimp kebab appetizers. Everywhere Josie turned was laughter and the tinkling of fine crystal and silver.

The event was like a featured magazine article, dreamed up by set and costume designers. Her silk ivory dress was so exquisitely tailored that it managed to hug her body in all of the right places, making her feel sexy instead of pregnant.

"Have I mentioned how gorgeous you look?" Dallas asked while his mom and Wren kept chatting.

"Not lately, but I'm always amenable to compliments."

The evening wound along without a hitch through dinner and Dallas's favorite key lime pie for dessert. After heartfelt toasts from Josie's maid of honor, Natalie, and Dallas's best man, Wyatt, came more dancing. Josie abandoned her agonizing heels on the seat of her chair in favor of going barefoot.

Midway through their dance, Bonnie came over, announcing that she'd like to dance with her father.

Exhausted, Josie was pleased to bow out.

She was also in need of a restroom, but since both downstairs powder rooms were in use, she headed upstairs to Dallas's room. It seemed surreal that the big, beautiful home would her hers, as well.

Eager to return to the party, she washed her hands, then surveyed her hair in the mirror.

Back in the bedroom, she paused to see if Dallas had cleared the dresser he'd promised she could use. Opening the top drawer, she found it brimming with socks and boxers. She'd changed her entire life, and he couldn't even bother cleaning a few drawers?

Suddenly the gravity of what she was on the verge of doing hit hard. She sat down on the bed, her mind and emotions whirling. Thinking that if Emma was looking down at her she might feel abandoned, Josie was consumed with grief. The crushing pain stemmed from so deep inside it was hard to breathe.

"Hey, gorgeous." She looked up to see Dallas enter the room. He looked every bit as handsome as ever—if not, more. Only now she realized how little she really knew him. "I've been looking for you. Apparently Mom has fireworks and she understandably doesn't want them to start without the bride."

"We need to talk."

"Sure," he said, taking her hands, urging her to her feet, "but let's make my mother happy first. You know how she gets, especially when it concerns a wedding."

"No, Dallas." Yanking her hands free, she scooted away from him. "You don't understand. There isn't going to be a wedding."

"What are you saying?"

"I can't let go. Emma needs me—if only to keep her memory alive."

"Honey," Dallas said, voice laced with concern, "are you even listening to yourself? You're not making sense."

"Seeing as how you couldn't even empty a sock drawer, neither does this marriage."

"WANT TO HELP ME WITH A FEW hundred calls?" Georgina asked Dallas Saturday morning. "While you were still puking whiskey, Josie called bright and early, apologizing and telling me that she'd call all of her guests, informing them that there isn't going to be a wedding. Well, you know what I say to that?"

"Can't imagine," he said, head feeling as if one of Cash's bulls had stomped it.

"Horse manure. I've got a lot of time and money invested in this wedding, and by God, if I have to drag you two to the altar kicking and screaming, that's what I'll do."

"I had enough dramatics last night." Fishing aspirin from the medicine drawer, he chewed four and swallowed.

"Not enough to get your head out of your behind. Josie's understandably terrified. You should've reassured her. Held her through the night."

"Please stop." Sitting at the counter, he willed her to vanish from his life and prosper elsewhere.

"I'm just getting started. For years, I've watched you spoil those girls rotten and focus anything left on this ranch. When you met Josie, for the first time since Bobbie Jo passed, you've seemed truly alive. You've even done the impossible and wrangled in your kids. Josie was the answer to our prayers. She wasn't afraid to not only tell you how it is with your girls, but show you. And after that, she even worked her magic on you. Now you're going to let her get away when what she needs is reassurance and your loving support?"

"Dammit all, Mom, I'd appreciate you staying the hell out of my business." He held his aching head in his hands.

His mother glared at him and left the room.

Only when she took off up the back staircase did

he finally dare relax. Lord, but she was a hot thorn in his side.

"Oh," she shouted down the stairs, "lest you think I'm canceling this Hollywood-worthy event, you've got another thing coming. Get up off of your derriere and get your bride back here by seven o'clock sharp."

JUST WHEN JOSIE THOUGHT she didn't have enough liquid in her to cry anymore, tears started up again.

"Please, eat," Nat urged Saturday morning. "You need your energy. We have a long day ahead of us, calling all of your guests and returning presents."

"I know," Josie said.

"While you were in the shower," Natalie said, hovering like a mother hen, "I called Georgina and she was not only understanding, but concerned."

"That's because she knows I'm right. This wedding came about way too fast."

Natalie set a glass of orange juice alongside Josie's scrambled cheesy eggs and toast.

The doorbell rang.

Josie groaned.

"I'll get it." Natalie headed for the front door.

When Josie heard a commotion in the foyer, her stomach fell. How was she supposed to forget she'd ever met Dallas Buckhorn when he was at that very moment, striding his way down the hall?

"I've, um, got errands," Nat said, taking her purse and keys before bolting outside.

"Hey." With a night's stubble and sleep-tousled hair, Dallas looked heartbreakingly handsome. With every breath in Josie's body, she now knew she loved him. She just didn't trust herself to know if in marrying him, she'd be doing the right thing. He held a pitifully wrapped package out to her. "I planned on saving this for tonight, but figure it might do me more good now."

"Thank you." She took the box from him only to set it on the entry-hall table. "But the wedding's still off. I can't just ride into the sunset with so much pain remaining in my past."

Hands fisted, he made a guttural growl. "Ham on a cupcake, woman, you frustrate the hell out of me. You don't think I have a few issues of my own? That's what marriage is—the two of us coming together to heal each other."

"I get that," she snapped, arms tightly folded, "but none of that changes how I feel. Don't you understand that once your husband betrays you to the tune of killing your child—even if it was an accident, it still tends to sting? Now I'm supposed to happily skip down Bridal Lane all over again? I can't even begin to describe how Hugh's suicide destroyed me. Then, when my own mother declared I was the cause for every tragedy that's happened…" Josie broke down, releasing years of grief in great, racking sobs.

Dallas didn't care that she tried pushing him away, he held her through the worst of it, until she was too exhausted to do anything but cling to his arms.

"I brought you something else that was supposed to have been a surprise." He kissed the top of her head. "You'll no doubt be mad at me for this, too, but before *we* can be whole, you need to be whole."

"There isn't going to be a *we*," she insisted through more sniffles.

"I know, but just sit tight for a few minutes. I have a feeling someone else is at the door." He went outside, a few minutes later returning, pulling someone behind him.

Josie's mother.

"I'm so sorry," her mom cried in a rush, running into her daughter's arms. "I said awful, unforgivable things to you. I was out of my mind. Losing little Em was unnatural. Grandparents don't bury their grandchildren."

"I know." Josie crushed her mother to her. In mere moments, years vanished, as did the pain. Yes, her mother had hurt her, but just as Josie had opened her heart to love again, she'd also learned to forgive.

"You've got a good man, here," her mom said with a nod to Dallas. "He flew every last one of us all the way out here from Maine. He had some harsh, much-deserved words for me, but nothing but love for you. Don't let him get away."

Holding out her hand to him, drawing Dallas into their circle, Josie simply said, "I won't."

AFTER SAYING THEIR VOWS and dancing and eating more cake than her barely fitting wedding dress could comfortably hold, Josie finally found herself cozy and warm in the guest cabin, nestled next to her husband of approximately five hours. In lieu of sexy lingerie, she wore roomy sweats and thick white socks.

In the morning, Henry was driving them to the Tulsa airport for a plane bound for a surprise exotic location

Dallas had promised would be warm. The girls were staying with his mom.

Her parents, brother and his wife and kids had already planned a return visit when Josie's baby was due.

"You're beautiful," Dallas said, cupping the side of her face. "Thank you for taking a chance on me—us." He kissed her. Softly. Sweetly. The way a husband tenderly kissed his beloved wife.

"Thank you for being strong enough to see me through…" Grasping his wrist, she kissed the palm of his hand. "Emma will always be in my heart. I just needed reminding that there's also plenty of room for you, the twins and our baby."

"Speaking of your daughter…" He reached beside the bed, drawing out the ragged gift he'd tried giving her that morning. "As you can see, gift wrapping's hardly my forte, but hopefully what's inside will more than make up for my lackluster presentation."

Intrigued, she scooted up in the bed, sitting cross-legged with his package on her lap.

With the paper gone, she lifted the flaps of an equally ugly box. Upon looking inside, she gasped. Looked at Dallas. Back to the box. "No…" Hands over trembling lips, eyes stinging with happy tears, she dared ask, "Is it really hers?"

Swallowing back his own tears, he nodded. "Henry ran this place for days while I searched every flea market and antiques store between here and Oklahoma City."

Nestled on a bed of pale pink satin was Emma's silver tea set. Lifting the delicately filigreed pot, she read the inscription, *For our precious Emma on her third birthday. We'll love you forever and always, Mommy and Daddy.*

"Even though your daughter will always be in your heart," Dallas said, "I thought it important that a part of her also shares a prominent place in our home."

There were no words to describe the love swelling Josie's heart. In Dallas, she'd found a friend, confidant, champion and love. A gentleman cowboy through and through. Together, she now knew they'd weather any storm. Emerging from the darkest clouds to walk in endless sun.

* * * * *

*Daisy Buckhorn has a secret and
has been in hiding for years.
But the past catches up with her in
Laura Marie Altom's next book in
THE BUCKHORN RANCH miniseries
available in June 2011
wherever Harlequin books are sold.*

COMING NEXT MONTH

Available March 8, 2011

#1345 THE COMEBACK COWBOY
American Romance's Men of the West
Cathy McDavid

#1346 THE DOCTOR'S FOREVER FAMILY
Forever, Texas
Marie Ferrarella

#1347 SECOND CHANCE DAD
Fatherhood
Pamela Stone

#1348 THE RELUCTANT BRIDE
Anne Marie Duquette

REQUEST YOUR FREE BOOKS!

2 FREE NOVELS PLUS 2 FREE GIFTS!

LOVE, HOME & HAPPINESS

YES! Please send me 2 FREE Harlequin American Romance® novels and my 2 FREE gifts (gifts are worth about $10). After receiving them, if I don't wish to receive any more books, I can return the shipping statement marked "cancel." If I don't cancel, I will receive 4 brand-new novels every month and be billed just $4.24 per book in the U.S. or $4.99 per book in Canada. That's a saving of at least 15% off the cover price! It's quite a bargain! Shipping and handling is just 50¢ per book in the U.S. and 75¢ per book in Canada.* I understand that accepting the 2 free books and gifts places me under no obligation to buy anything. I can always return a shipment and cancel at any time. Even if I never buy another book, the two free books and gifts are mine to keep forever.

154/354 HDN FDKS

Name _____ (PLEASE PRINT) _____

Address _____ Apt. # _____

City _____ State/Prov. _____ Zip/Postal Code _____

Signature (if under 18, a parent or guardian must sign)

Mail to the **Reader Service:**
IN U.S.A.: P.O. Box 1867, Buffalo, NY 14240-1867
IN CANADA: P.O. Box 609, Fort Erie, Ontario L2A 5X3

Not valid for current subscribers to Harlequin American Romance books.

Want to try two free books from another line?
Call 1-800-873-8635 or visit www.ReaderService.com.

* Terms and prices subject to change without notice. Prices do not include applicable taxes. Sales tax applicable in N.Y. Canadian residents will be charged applicable taxes. Offer not valid in Quebec. This offer is limited to one order per household. All orders subject to credit approval. Credit or debit balances in a customer's account(s) may be offset by any other outstanding balance owed by or to the customer. Please allow 4 to 6 weeks for delivery. Offer available while quantities last.

Your Privacy—The Reader Service is committed to protecting your privacy. Our Privacy Policy is available online at www.ReaderService.com or upon request from the Reader Service.

We make a portion of our mailing list available to reputable third parties that offer products we believe may interest you. If you prefer that we not exchange your name with third parties, or if you wish to clarify or modify your communication preferences, please visit us at www.ReaderService.com/consumerschoice or write to us at Reader Service Preference Service, P.O. Box 9062, Buffalo, NY 14269. Include your complete name and address.

USA TODAY *bestselling author Lynne Graham*
is back with a thrilling new trilogy
SECRETLY PREGNANT, CONVENIENTLY WED

*Three heroines must marry alpha males to keep
their dreams...but Alejandro, Angelo and Cesario
are not about to be tamed!*

Book 1—JEMIMA'S SECRET
Available March 2011 from Harlequin Presents®.

JEMIMA yanked open a drawer in the sideboard to find Alfie's birth certificate. Her son was her husband's child. It was a question of telling the truth whether she liked it or not. She extended the certificate to Alejandro.

"This has to be nonsense," Alejandro asserted.

"Well, if you can find some other way of explaining how I managed to give birth by that date and Alfie not be yours, I'd like to hear it," Jemima challenged.

Alejandro glanced up, golden eyes bright as blades and as dangerous. "All this proves is that you must still have been pregnant when you walked out on our marriage. It does not automatically follow that the child is mine."

"'I know it doesn't suit you to hear this news now and I really didn't want to tell you. But I can't lie to you about it. Someday Alfie may want to look you up and get acquainted."

"If what you have just told me is the truth, if that little boy does prove to be mine, it was vindictive and extremely selfish of you to leave me in ignorance!"

Jemima paled. "When I left you, I had no idea that I was still pregnant."

"Two years is a long period of time, yet you made no attempt to inform me that I might be a father. I will want DNA tests to confirm your claim before I make any decision about what I want to do."

"Do as you like," she told him curtly. "*I* know who Alfie's father is and there has never been any doubt of his identity."

"I will make arrangements for the tests to be carried out and I will see you again when the result is available," Alejandro drawled with lashings of dark Spanish masculine reserve.

"I'll contact a solicitor and start the divorce," Jemima proffered in turn.

Alejandro's eyes narrowed in a piercing scrutiny that made her uncomfortable. "It would be foolish to do anything before we have that DNA result."

"I disagree," Jemima flashed back. "I should have applied for a divorce the minute I left you!"

Alejandro quirked an ebony brow. "And why didn't you?"

Jemima dealt him a fulminating glance but said nothing, merely moving past him to open her front door in a blunt invitation for him to leave.

"I'll be in touch," he delivered on the doorstep.

What is Alejandro's next move? Perhaps rekindling their marriage is the only solution! But will Jemima agree?

Find out in Lynne Graham's
exciting new romance
JEMIMA'S SECRET

Available March 2011
from Harlequin Presents®.

Start your Best Body today with these top 3 nutrition tips!

1. **SHOP THE PERIMETER OF THE GROCERY STORE:** The good stuff—fruits, veggies, lean proteins and dairy—always line the outer edges of the store. When you veer into the center aisles, you enter the temptation zone, where the unhealthy foods live.

2. **WATCH PORTION SIZES:** Most portion sizes in restaurants are nearly twice the size of a true serving and at home, it's easy to "clean your plate." Use these easy serving guidelines:
   - Protein: the palm of your hand
   - Grains or Fruit: a cup of your hand
   - Veggies: the palm of two open hands

3. **USE THE RAINBOW RULE FOR PRODUCE:** Your produce drawers should be filled with every color of fruits and vegetables. The greater the variety, the more vitamins and other nutrients you add to your diet.

Find these and many more helpful tips in

YOUR BEST BODY NOW
by
TOSCA RENO
WITH STACY BAKER

Bestselling Author of
THE EAT-CLEAN DIET

Available wherever books are sold!

PRESENTING... THE SEVENTH ANNUAL
MORE THAN WORDS™ ANTHOLOGY

Five bestselling authors
Five real-life heroines

This year's Harlequin
More Than Words award
recipients have changed lives,
one good deed at a time. To
celebrate these real-life heroines,
some of Harlequin's most
acclaimed authors have honored
the winners by writing stories
inspired by these dedicated
women. Within the pages
of *More Than Words Volume 7*,
you will find novellas written
by Carly Phillips, Donna Hill
and Jill Shalvis—and online at
www.HarlequinMoreThanWords.com
you can also access stories by
Pamela Morsi and Meryl Sawyer.

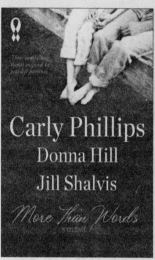

Coming soon in print and online!

Visit
www.HarlequinMoreThanWords.com
to access your FREE ebooks and to nominate
a real-life heroine in your community.

Proceeds from the sale of this book will be
reinvested in Harlequin's charitable initiatives.